LEGO NINJAGO
Masters of Spinjitzu

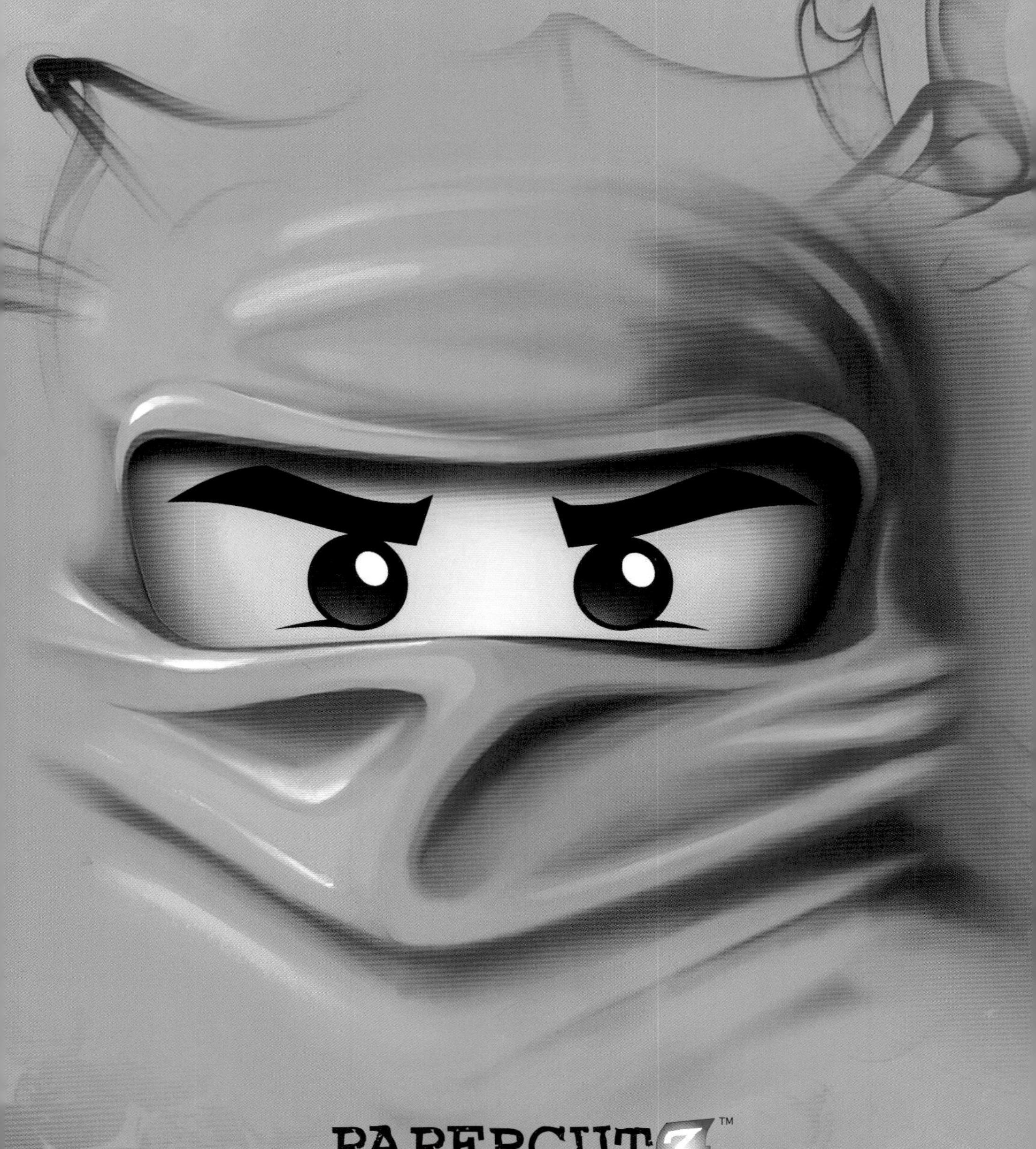

PAPERCUTZ™

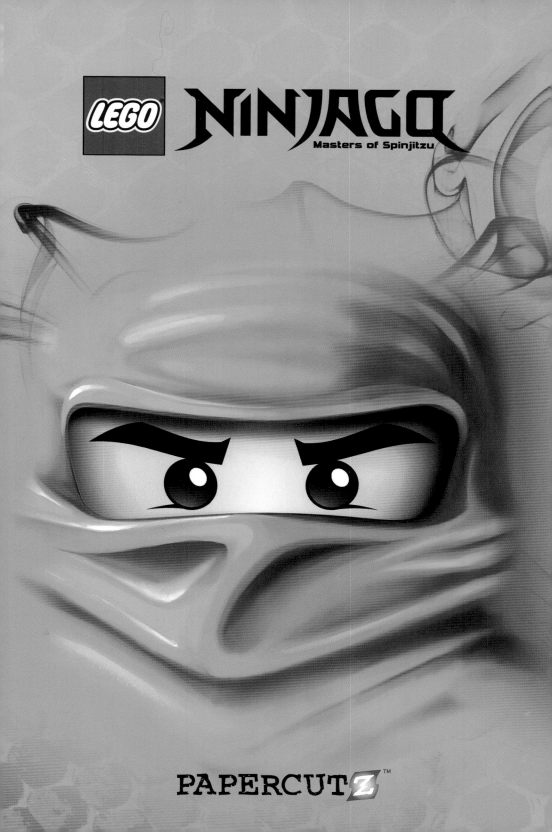

LEGO NINJAGO
Masters of Spinjitzu

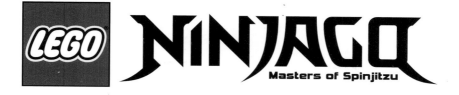

#5 "KINGDOM OF THE SNAKES"

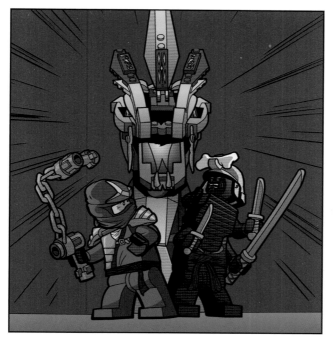

Greg Farshtey – Writer
Jolyon Yates – Artist
Jayjay Jackson – Colorist
Paul Lee – Cover Artist
Laurie E. Smith – Cover Colorist

PAPERCUTZ
New York

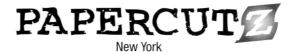

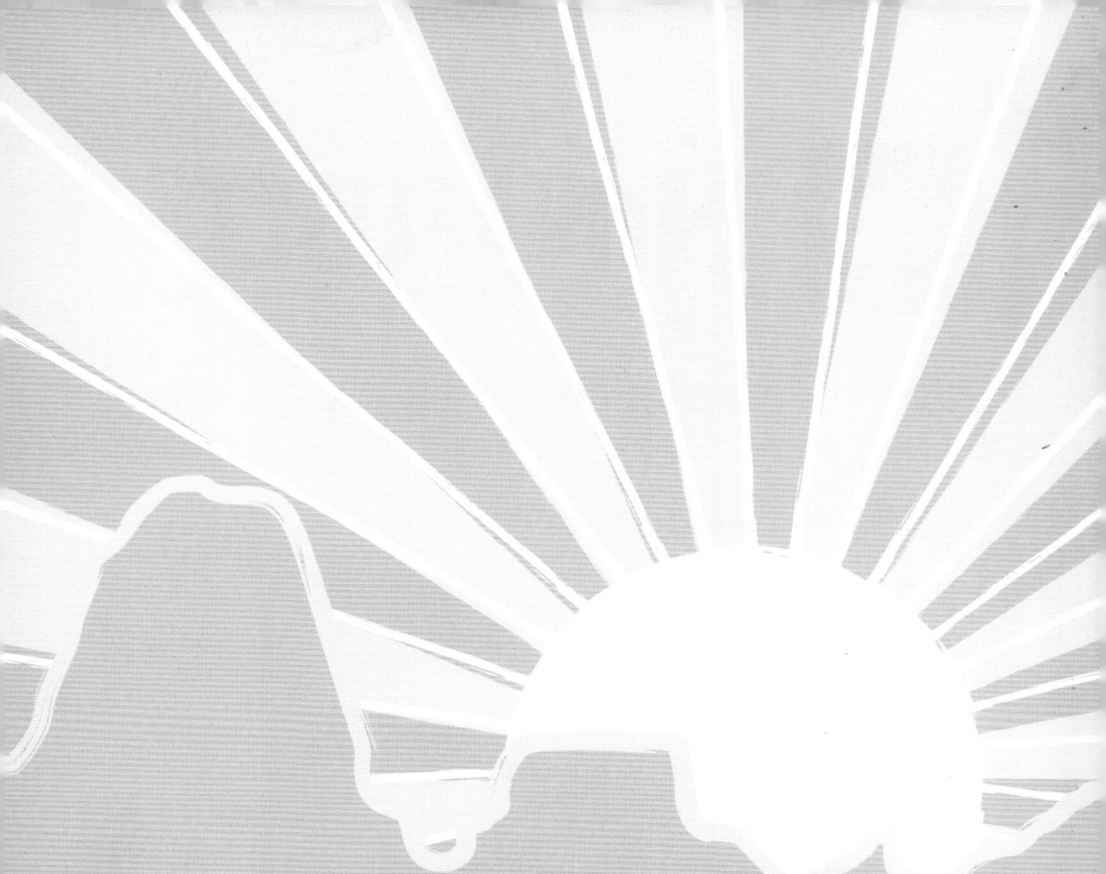

LEGO® NINJAGO Masters of Spinjitzu
#5 "Kingdom of the Snakes"

GREG FARSHTEY – Writer
JOLYON YATES – Artist
JAYJAY JACKSON – Colorist
BRYAN SENKA – Letterer
Production by NELSON DESIGN GROUP, LLC
Special thanks to JACK "KING" KIRBY
Associate Editor – MICHAEL PETRANEK
JIM SALICRUP
Editor-in-Chief

ISBN: 978-1-59707-356-1 paperback edition
ISBN: 978-1-59707-357-8 hardcover edition

Printed in US
October 2012 by Lifetouch Printing
5126 Forest Hills Ct
Loves Park, IL 61111

Distributed by Macmillan

First Printing

MEET THE MASTERS OF SPINJITZU...

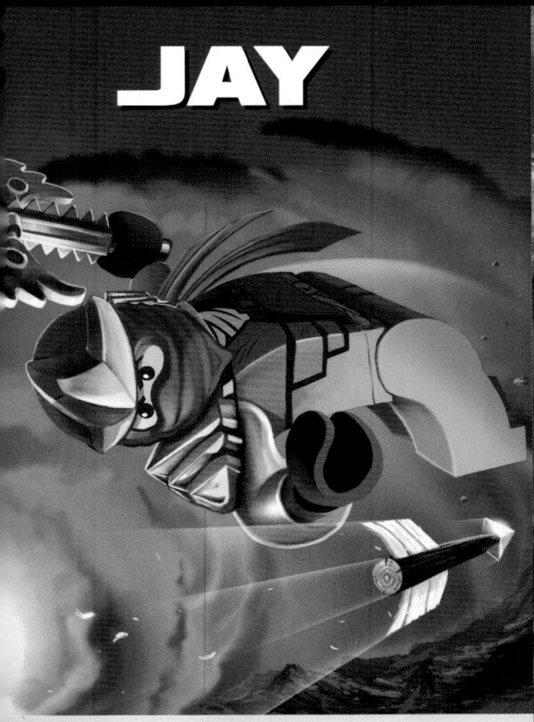
JAY

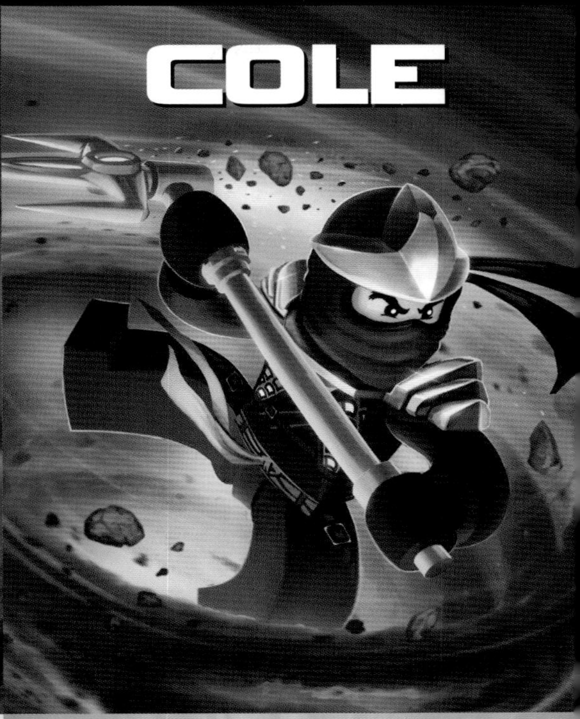
COLE

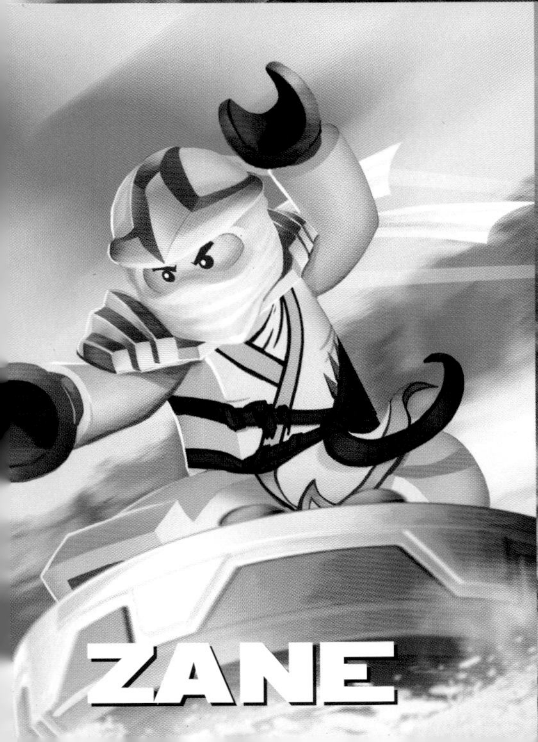
ZANE

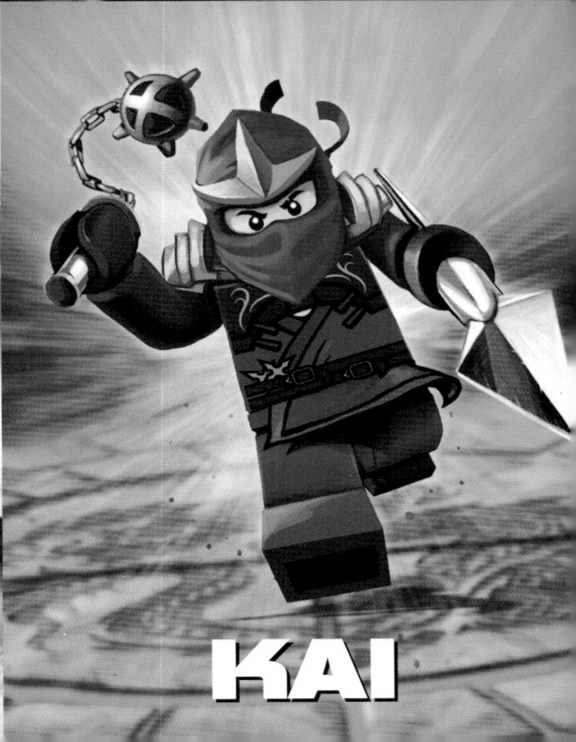
KAI

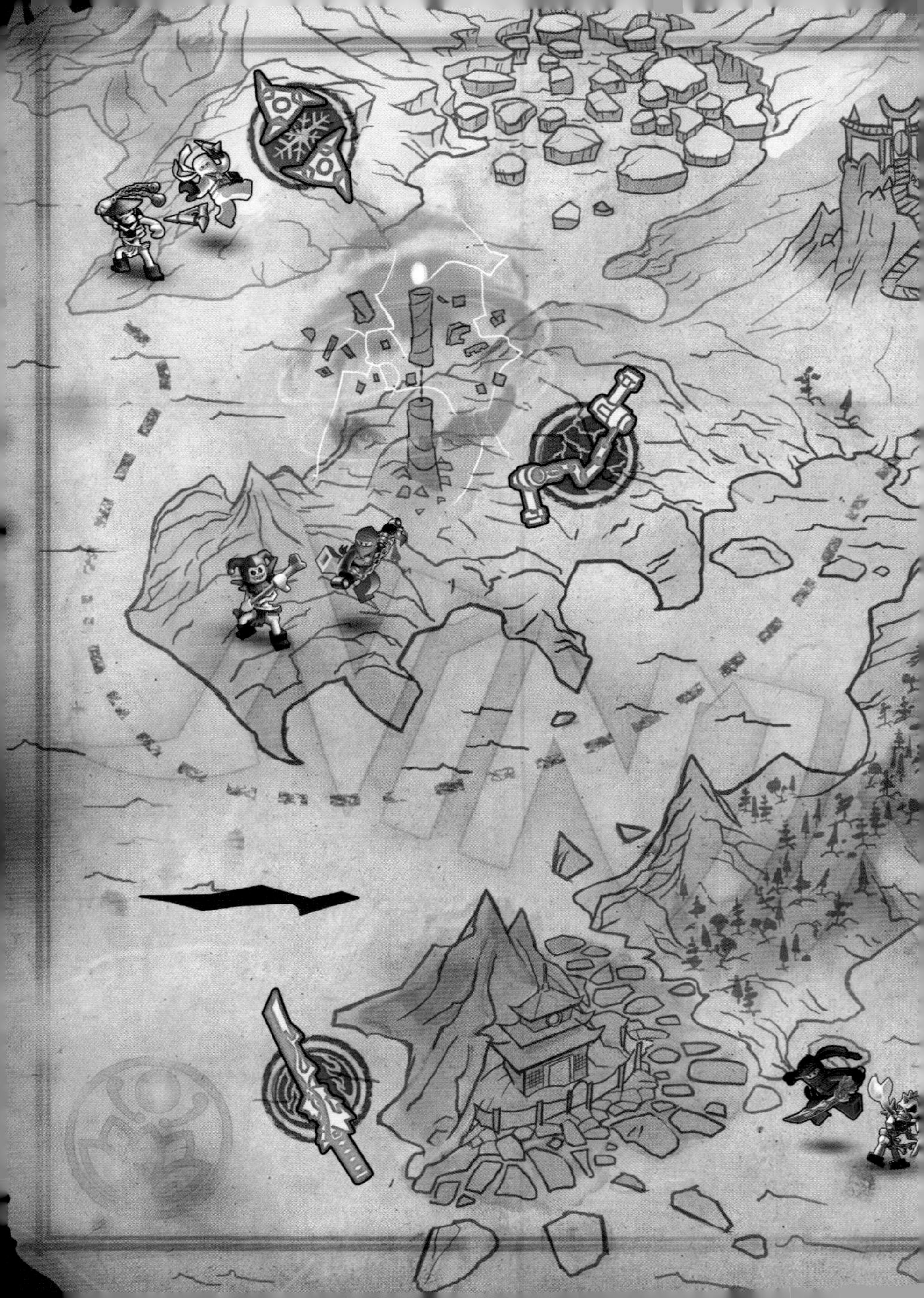

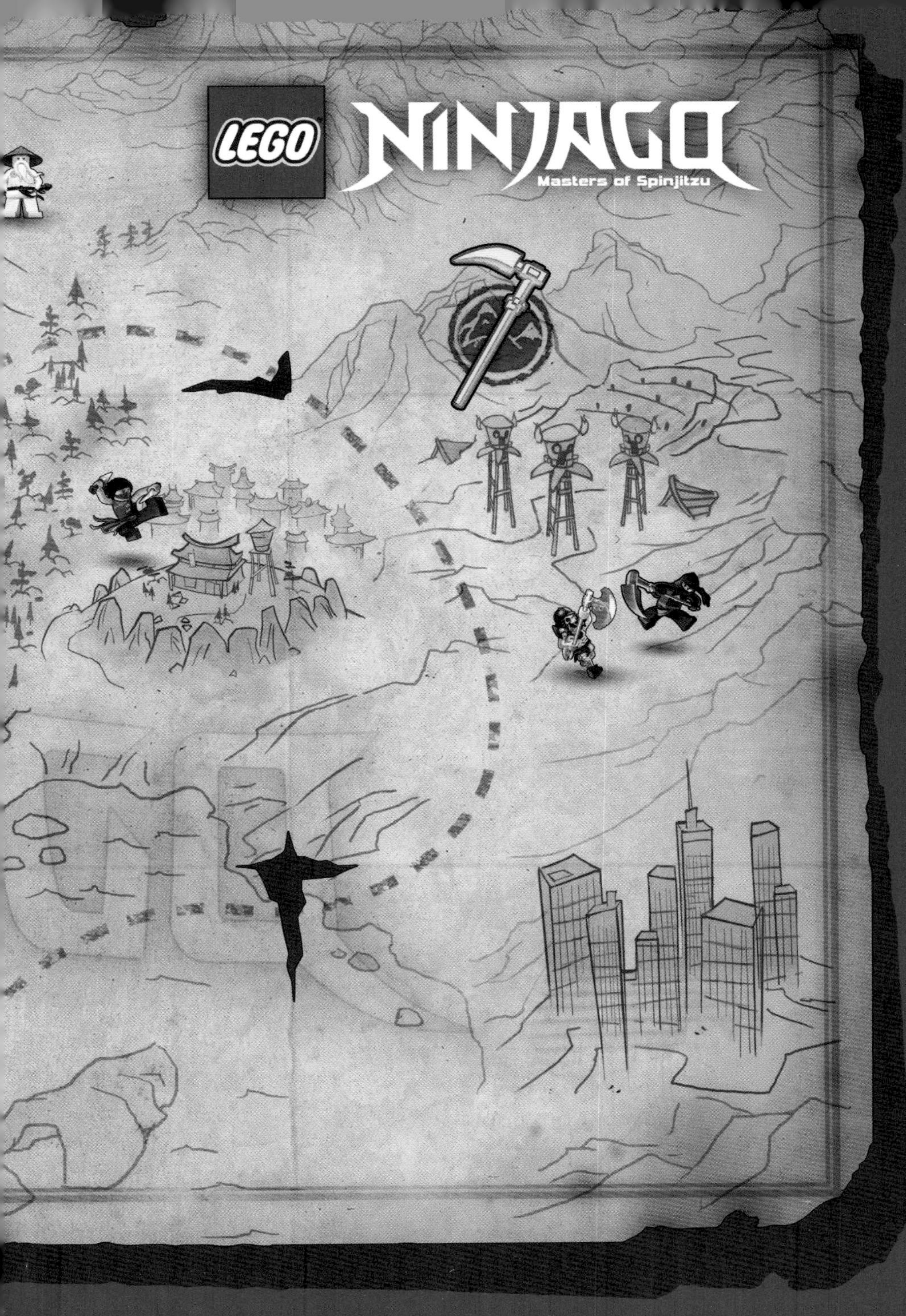
LEGO
NINJAGO
Masters of Spinjitzu

And the Master of the Masters of Spinjitzu...

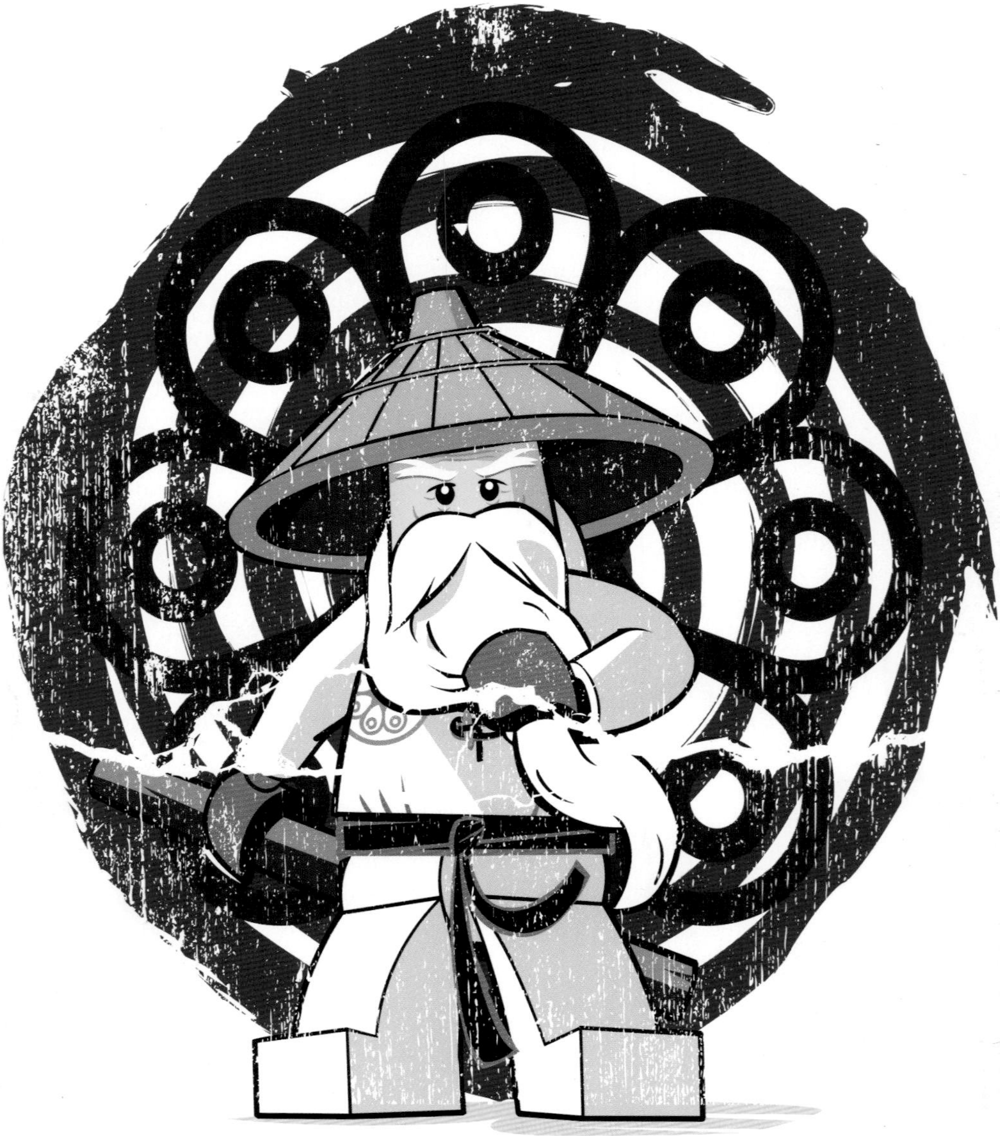

SENSEI WU

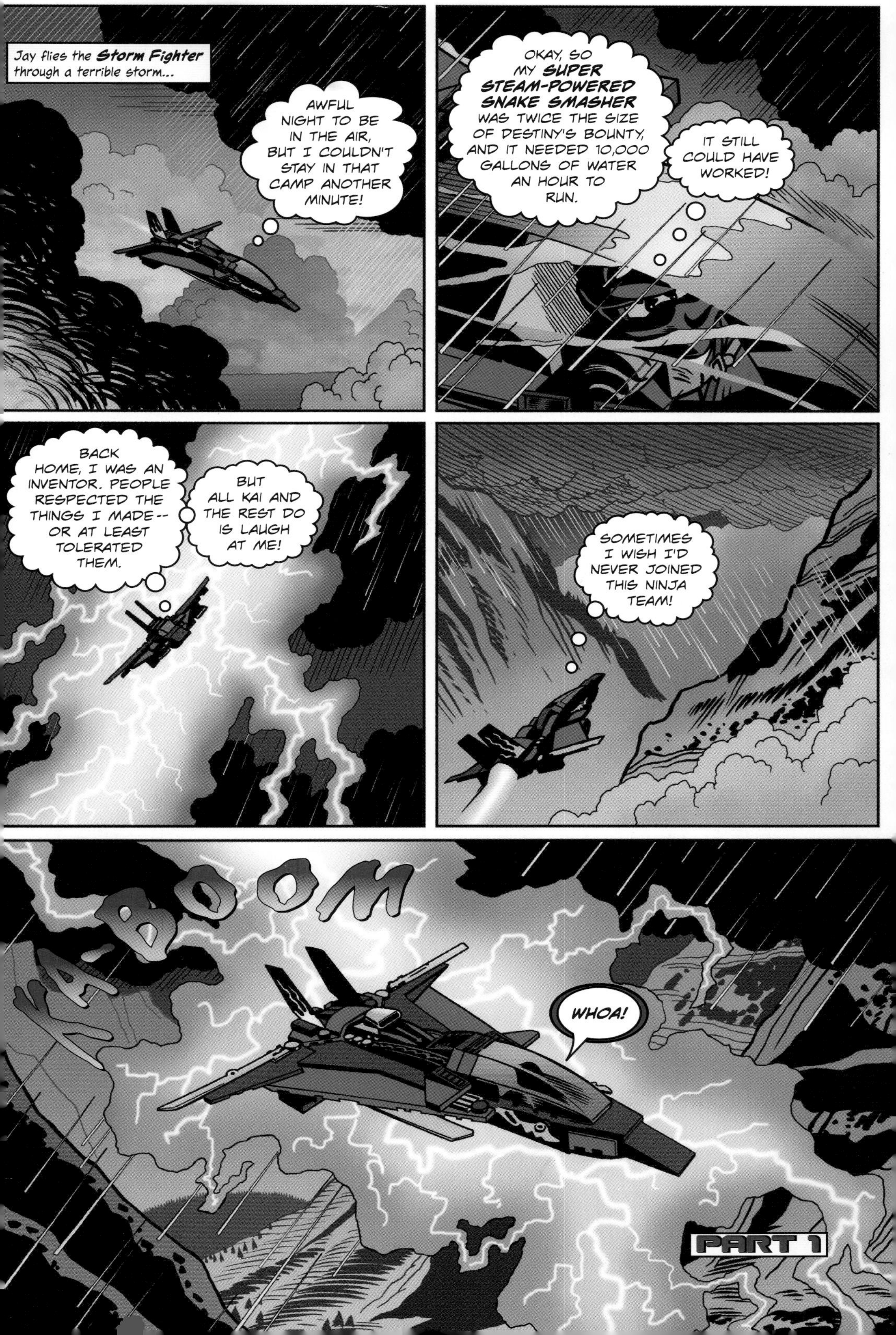
Jay flies the Storm Fighter through a terrible storm...
AWFUL NIGHT TO BE IN THE AIR, BUT I COULDN'T STAY IN THAT CAMP ANOTHER MINUTE!
OKAY, SO MY SUPER STEAM-POWERED SNAKE SMASHER WAS TWICE THE SIZE OF DESTINY'S BOUNTY, AND IT NEEDED 10,000 GALLONS OF WATER AN HOUR TO RUN.
IT STILL COULD HAVE WORKED!
BACK HOME, I WAS AN INVENTOR. PEOPLE RESPECTED THE THINGS I MADE-- OR AT LEAST TOLERATED THEM.
BUT ALL KAI AND THE REST DO IS LAUGH AT ME!
SOMETIMES I WISH I'D NEVER JOINED THIS NINJA TEAM!
KABOOM
WHOA!
PART 1

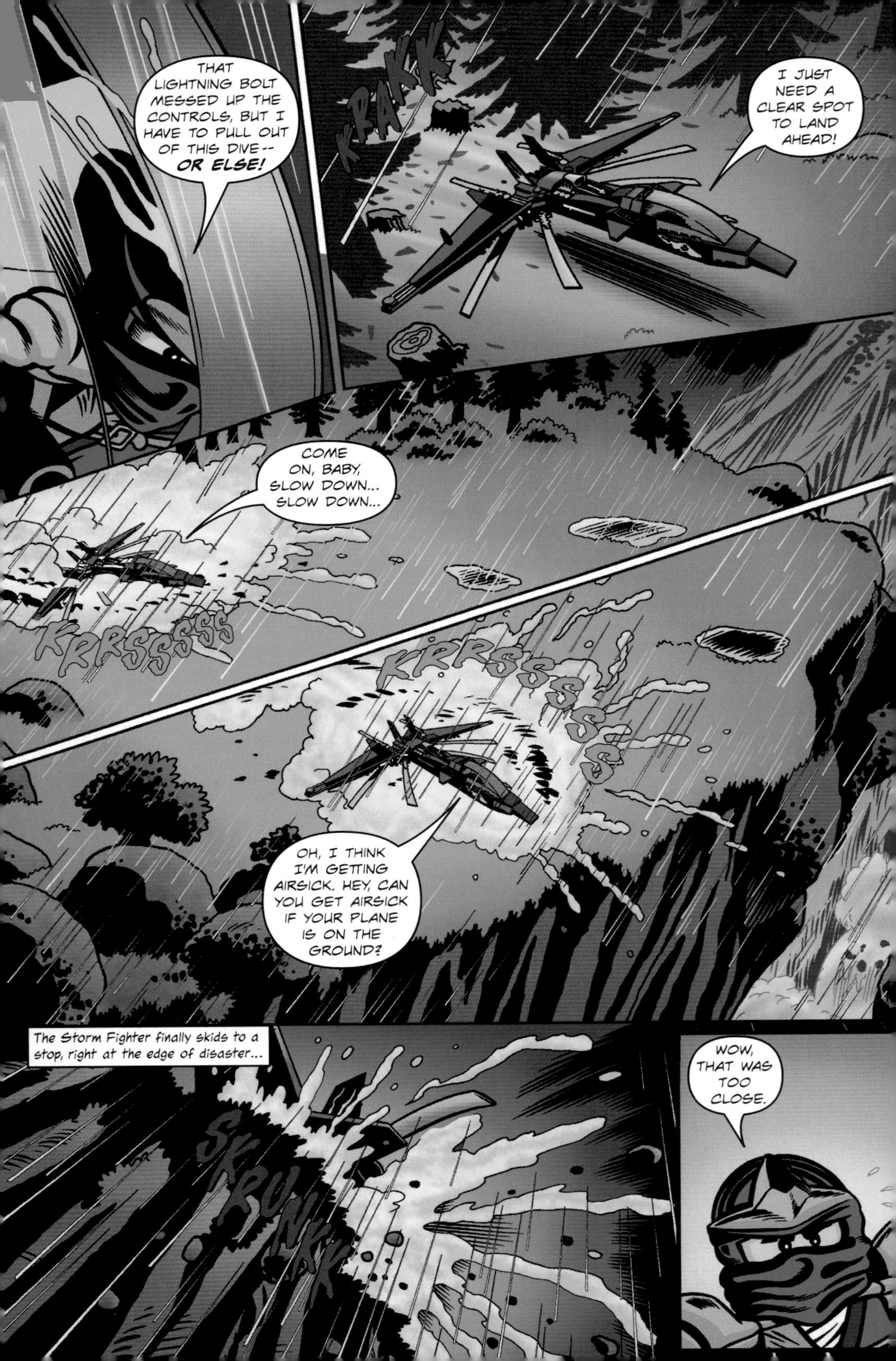
THAT LIGHTNING BOLT MESSED UP THE CONTROLS, BUT I HAVE TO PULL OUT OF THIS DIVE-- **OR ELSE!**
KRAKK
I JUST NEED A CLEAR SPOT TO LAND AHEAD!
COME ON, BABY, SLOW DOWN... SLOW DOWN...
KRRSSSSSS
KRRSSSSSS
OH, I THINK I'M GETTING AIRSICK. HEY, CAN YOU GET AIRSICK IF YOUR PLANE IS ON THE GROUND?
The Storm Fighter finally skids to a stop, right at the edge of disaster...
SKRUNKK
WOW, THAT WAS TOO CLOSE.

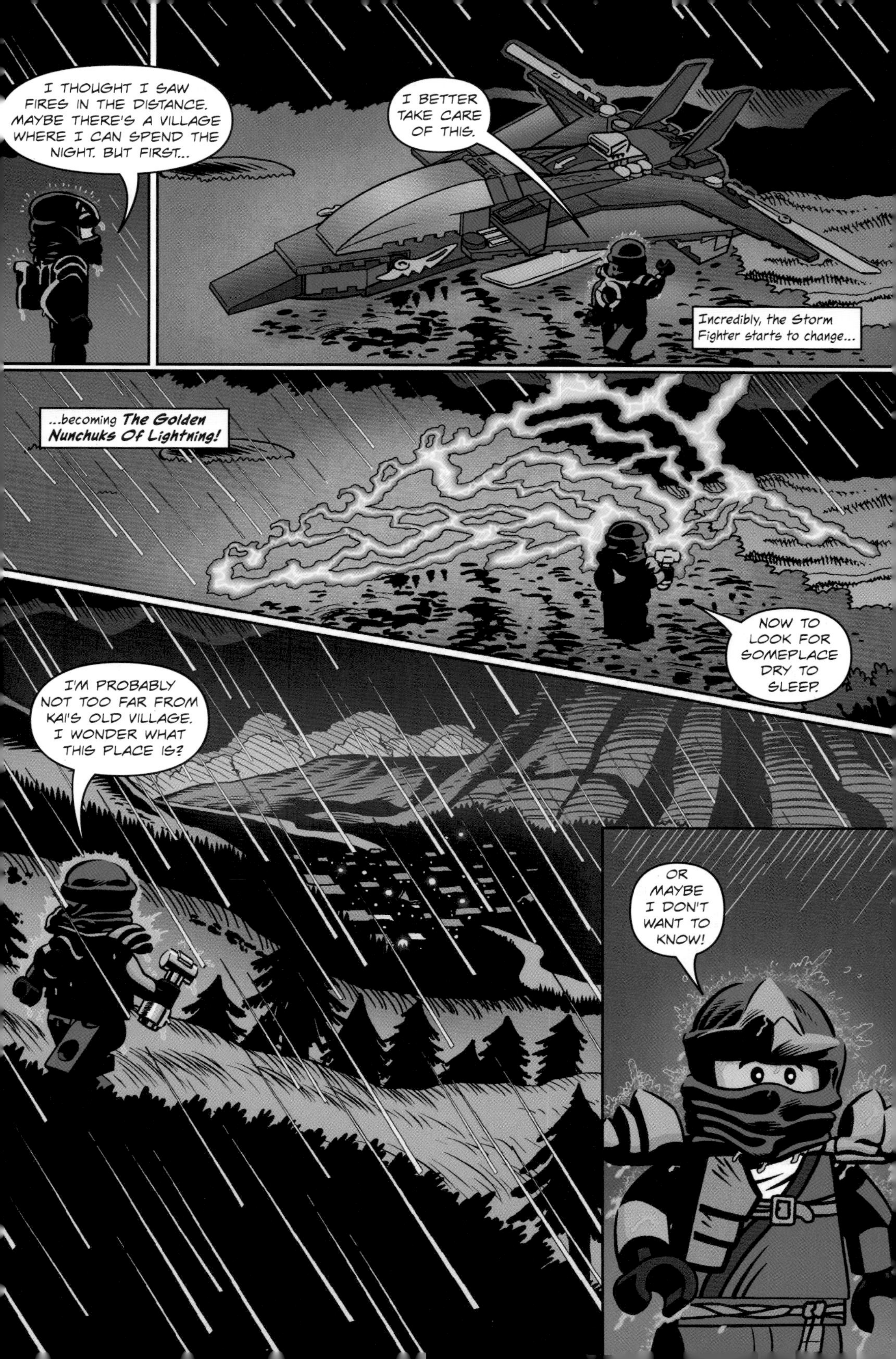
I THOUGHT I SAW FIRES IN THE DISTANCE. MAYBE THERE'S A VILLAGE WHERE I CAN SPEND THE NIGHT. BUT FIRST...
I BETTER TAKE CARE OF THIS.
Incredibly, the Storm Fighter starts to change...
...becoming The Golden Nunchuks Of Lightning!
NOW TO LOOK FOR SOMEPLACE DRY TO SLEEP.
I'M PROBABLY NOT TOO FAR FROM KAI'S OLD VILLAGE. I WONDER WHAT THIS PLACE IS?
OR MAYBE I DON'T WANT TO KNOW!

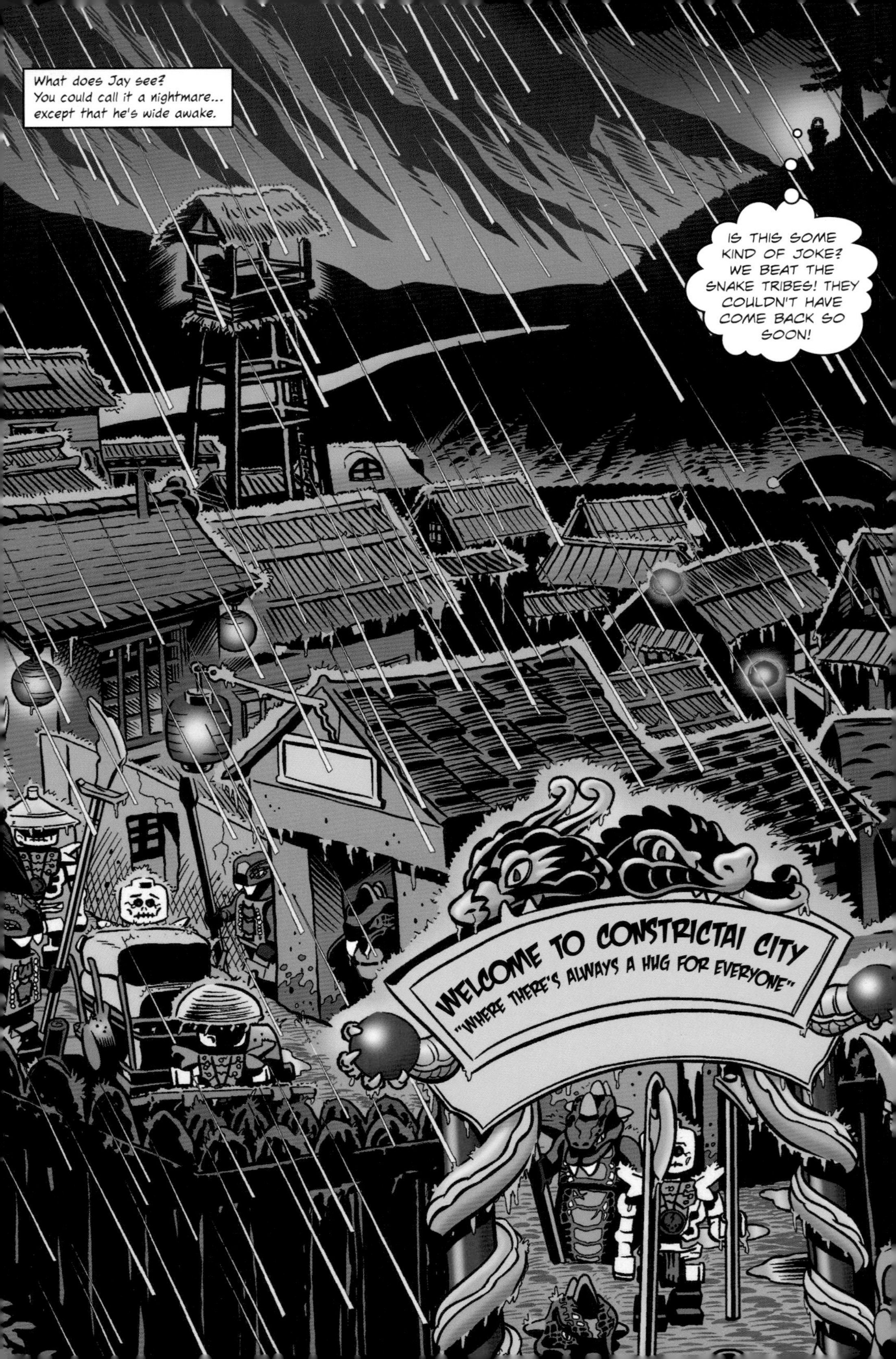
What does Jay see? You could call it a nightmare... except that he's wide awake.
IS THIS SOME KIND OF JOKE? WE BEAT THE SNAKE TRIBES! THEY COULDN'T HAVE COME BACK SO SOON!
WELCOME TO CONSTRICTAI CITY
"WHERE THERE'S ALWAYS A HUG FOR EVERYONE"

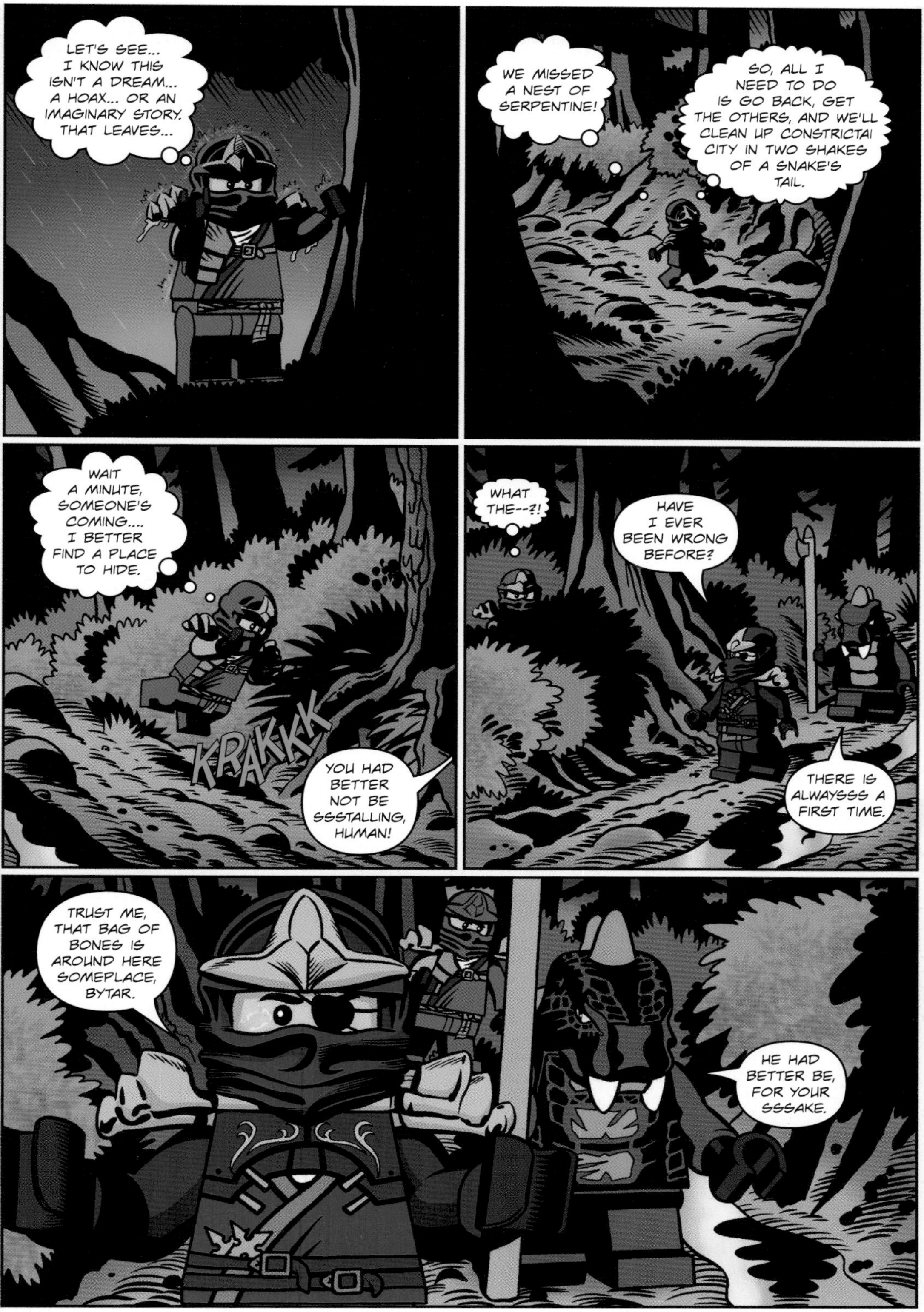
LET'S SEE... I KNOW THIS ISN'T A DREAM... A HOAX... OR AN IMAGINARY STORY. THAT LEAVES...
WE MISSED A NEST OF SERPENTINE!
SO, ALL I NEED TO DO IS GO BACK, GET THE OTHERS, AND WE'LL CLEAN UP CONSTRICTAI CITY IN TWO SHAKES OF A SNAKE'S TAIL.
WAIT A MINUTE, SOMEONE'S COMING.... I BETTER FIND A PLACE TO HIDE.
KRAKKK
YOU HAD BETTER NOT BE SSSTALLING, HUMAN!
WHAT THE--?!
HAVE I EVER BEEN WRONG BEFORE?
THERE IS ALWAYSSS A FIRST TIME.
TRUST ME, THAT BAG OF BONES IS AROUND HERE SOMEPLACE, BYTAR.
HE HAD BETTER BE, FOR YOUR SSSAKE.

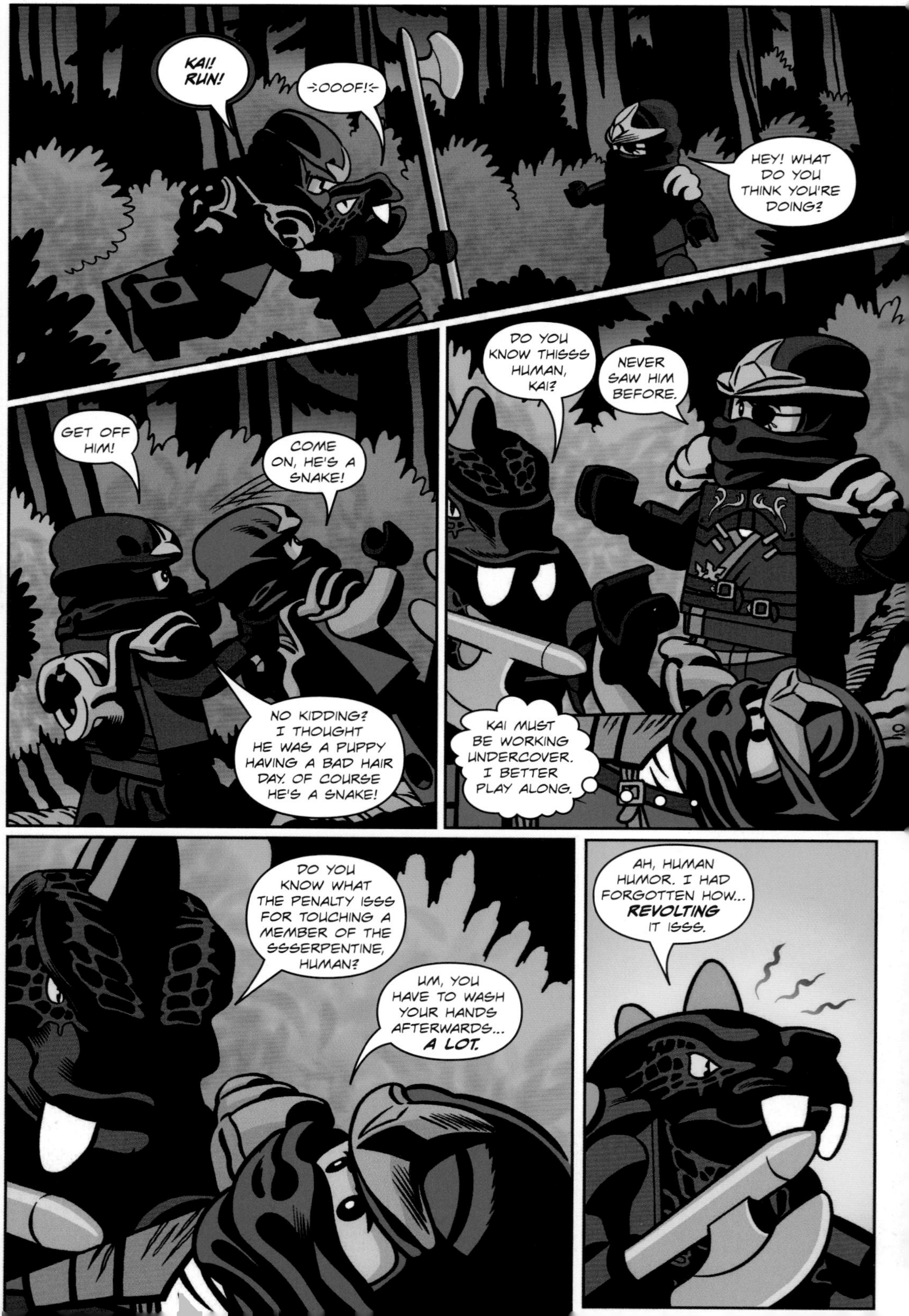
KAI! RUN!
OOOF!
HEY! WHAT DO YOU THINK YOU'RE DOING?
GET OFF HIM!
COME ON, HE'S A SNAKE!
NO KIDDING? I THOUGHT HE WAS A PUPPY HAVING A BAD HAIR DAY. OF COURSE HE'S A SNAKE!
DO YOU KNOW THISSS HUMAN, KAI?
NEVER SAW HIM BEFORE.
KAI MUST BE WORKING UNDERCOVER. I BETTER PLAY ALONG.
DO YOU KNOW WHAT THE PENALTY ISSS FOR TOUCHING A MEMBER OF THE SSSERPENTINE, HUMAN?
UM, YOU HAVE TO WASH YOUR HANDS AFTERWARDS... A LOT.
AH, HUMAN HUMOR. I HAD FORGOTTEN HOW... REVOLTING IT ISSS.

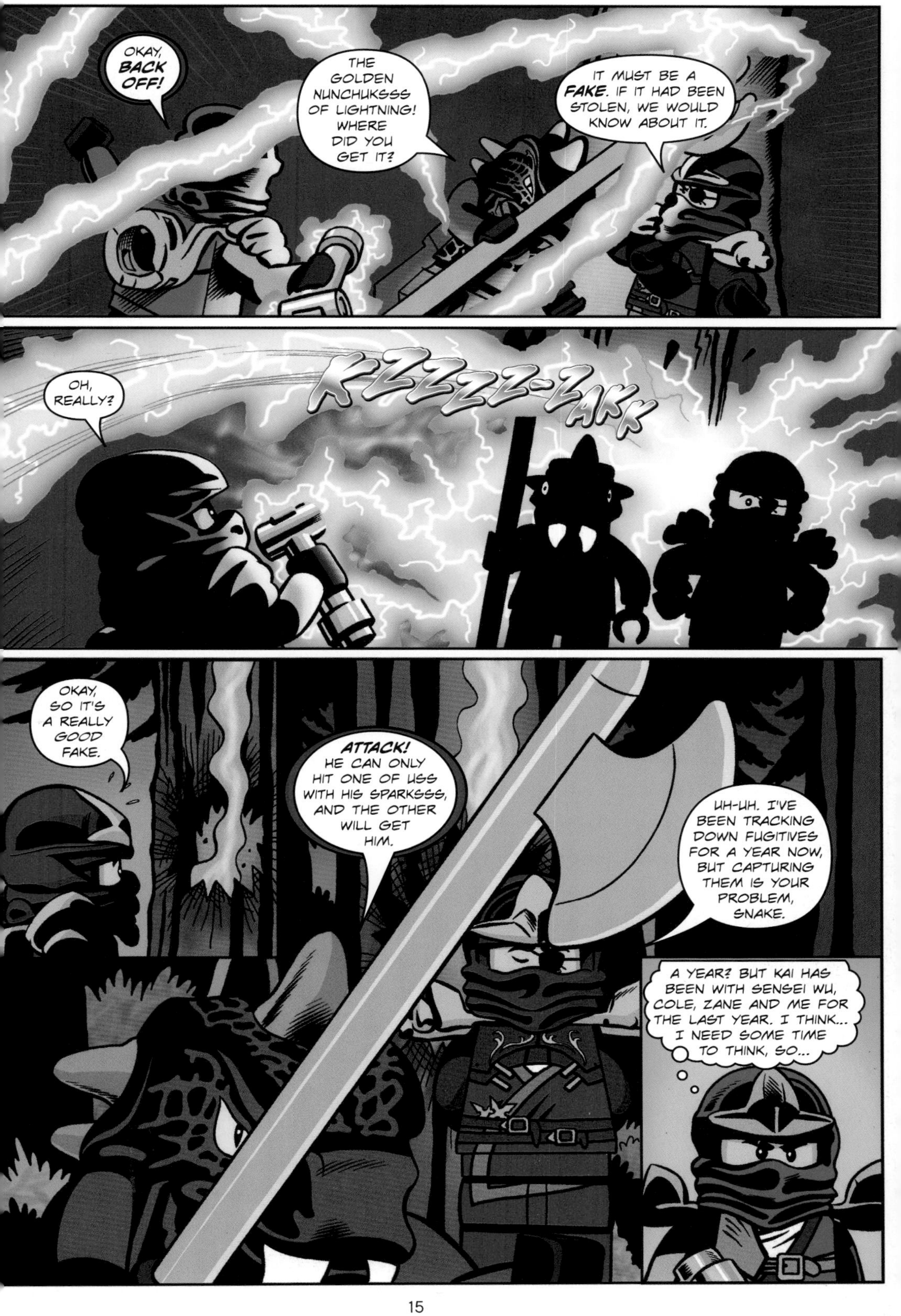
OKAY, BACK OFF!
THE GOLDEN NUNCHUKSSS OF LIGHTNING! WHERE DID YOU GET IT?
IT MUST BE A FAKE. IF IT HAD BEEN STOLEN, WE WOULD KNOW ABOUT IT.
OH, REALLY?
K-ZZZZZ-ZAKK
OKAY, SO IT'S A REALLY GOOD FAKE.
ATTACK! HE CAN ONLY HIT ONE OF USS WITH HIS SPARKSSS, AND THE OTHER WILL GET HIM.
UH-UH. I'VE BEEN TRACKING DOWN FUGITIVES FOR A YEAR NOW, BUT CAPTURING THEM IS YOUR PROBLEM, SNAKE.
A YEAR? BUT KAI HAS BEEN WITH SENSEI WU, COLE, ZANE AND ME FOR THE LAST YEAR. I THINK... I NEED SOME TIME TO THINK, SO...

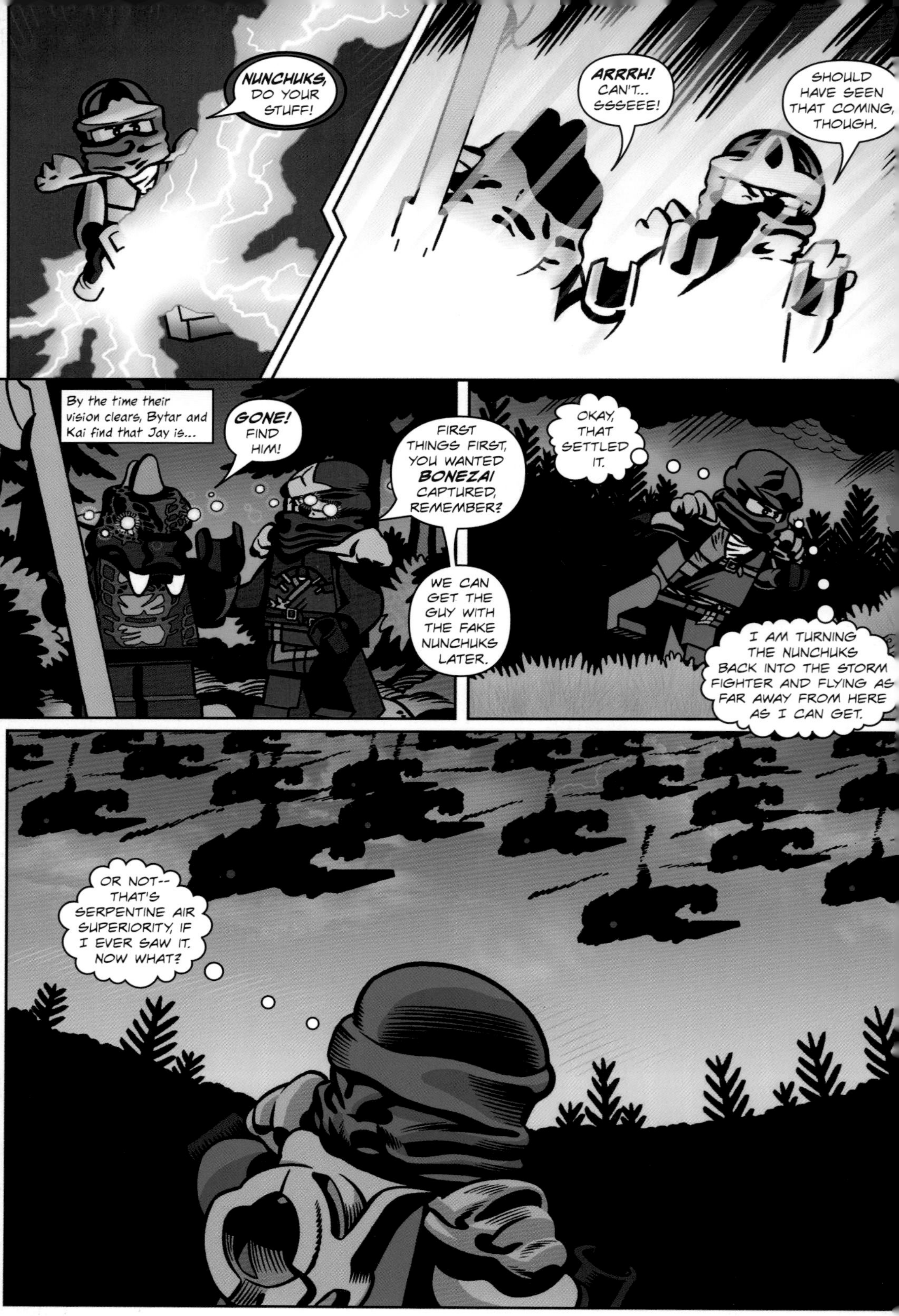
NUNCHUKS, DO YOUR STUFF!
ARRRH! CAN'T... SSSEEE!
SHOULD HAVE SEEN THAT COMING, THOUGH.
By the time their vision clears, Bytar and Kai find that Jay is...
GONE! FIND HIM!
FIRST THINGS FIRST, YOU WANTED BONEZAI CAPTURED, REMEMBER?
WE CAN GET THE GUY WITH THE FAKE NUNCHUKS LATER.
OKAY, THAT SETTLED IT.
I AM TURNING THE NUNCHUKS BACK INTO THE STORM FIGHTER AND FLYING AS FAR AWAY FROM HERE AS I CAN GET.
OR NOT-- THAT'S SERPENTINE AIR SUPERIORITY, IF I EVER SAW IT. NOW WHAT?

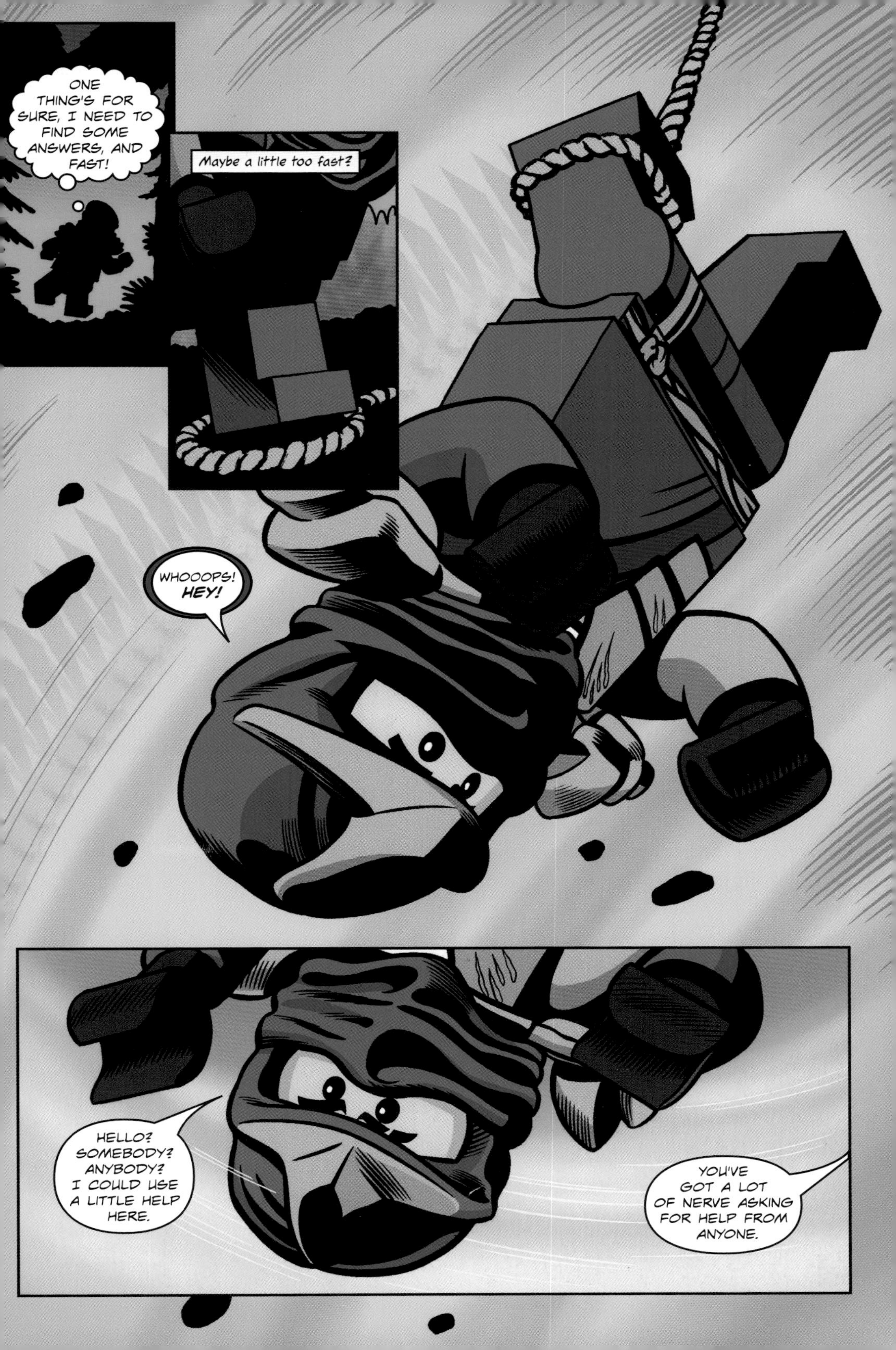

ONE THING'S FOR SURE, I NEED TO FIND SOME ANSWERS, AND FAST!
Maybe a little too fast?
WHOOOPS! HEY!
HELLO? SOMEBODY? ANYBODY? I COULD USE A LITTLE HELP HERE.
YOU'VE GOT A LOT OF NERVE ASKING FOR HELP FROM ANYONE.

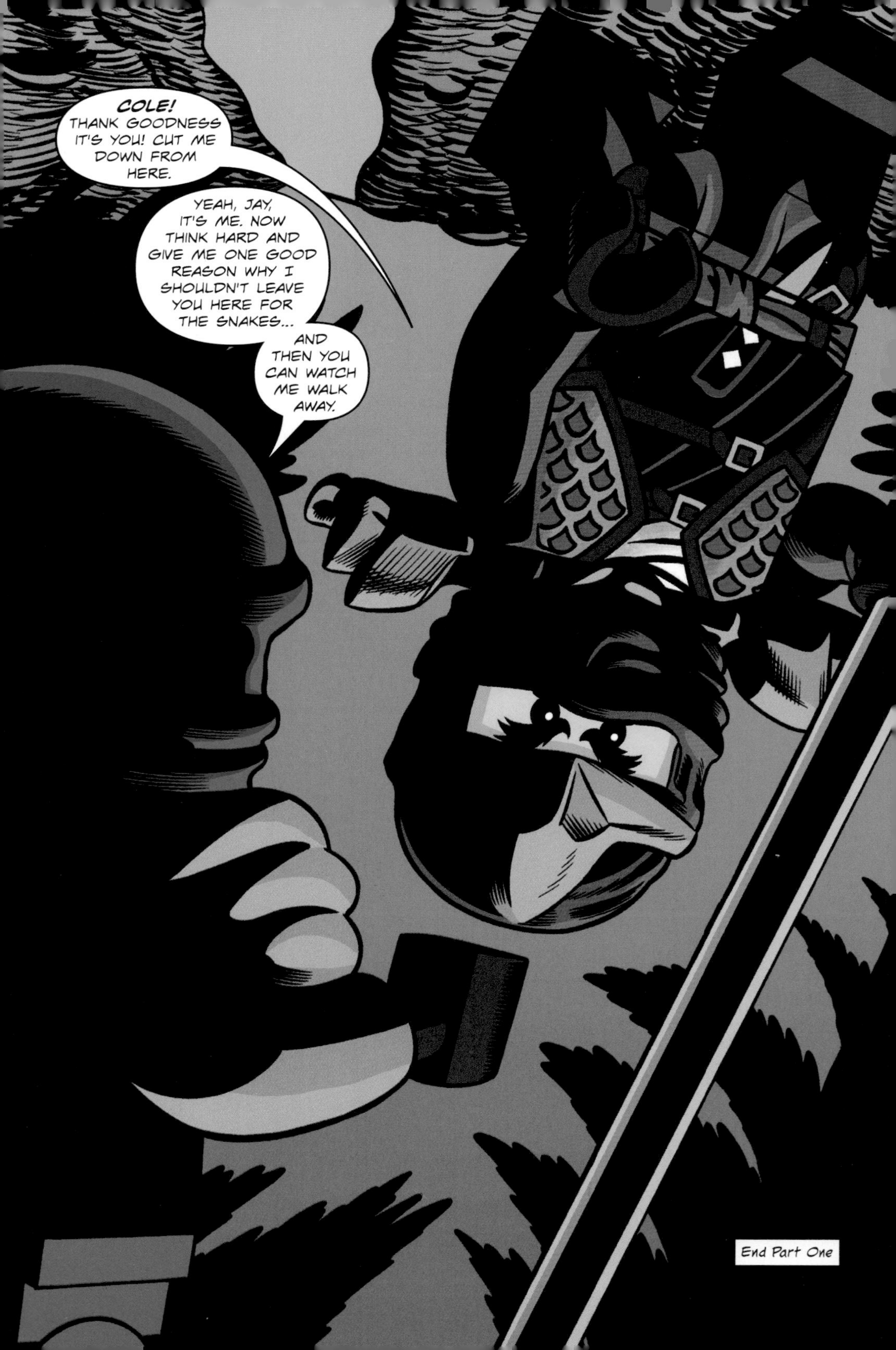
COLE! THANK GOODNESS IT'S YOU! CUT ME DOWN FROM HERE.
YEAH, JAY, IT'S ME. NOW THINK HARD AND GIVE ME ONE GOOD REASON WHY I SHOULDN'T LEAVE YOU HERE FOR THE SNAKES...
AND THEN YOU CAN WATCH ME WALK AWAY.
End Part One

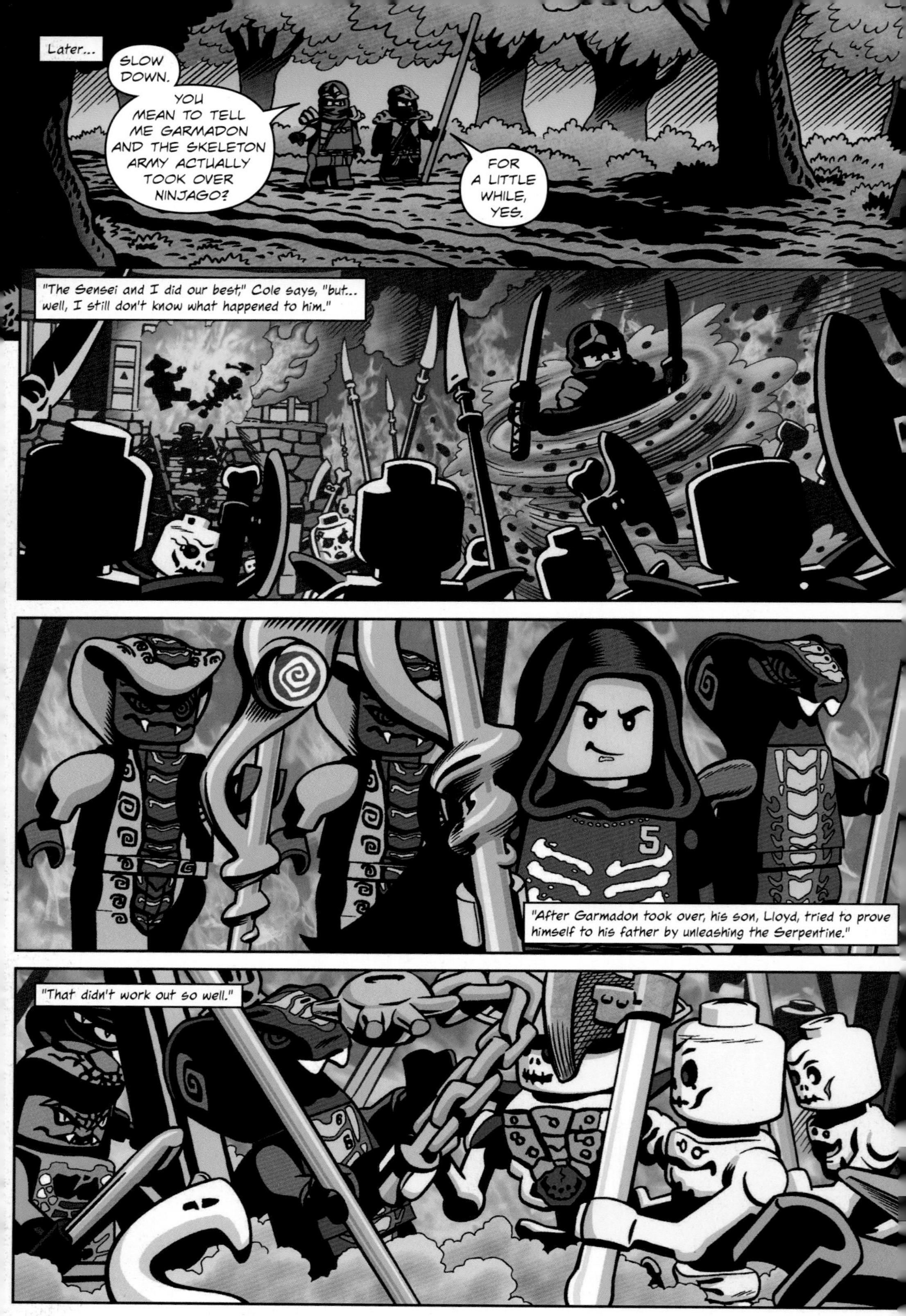
Later...
SLOW DOWN.
YOU MEAN TO TELL ME GARMADON AND THE SKELETON ARMY ACTUALLY TOOK OVER NINJAGO?
FOR A LITTLE WHILE, YES.
"The Sensei and I did our best," Cole says, "but... well, I still don't know what happened to him."
"After Garmadon took over, his son, Lloyd, tried to prove himself to his father by unleashing the Serpentine."
"That didn't work out so well."

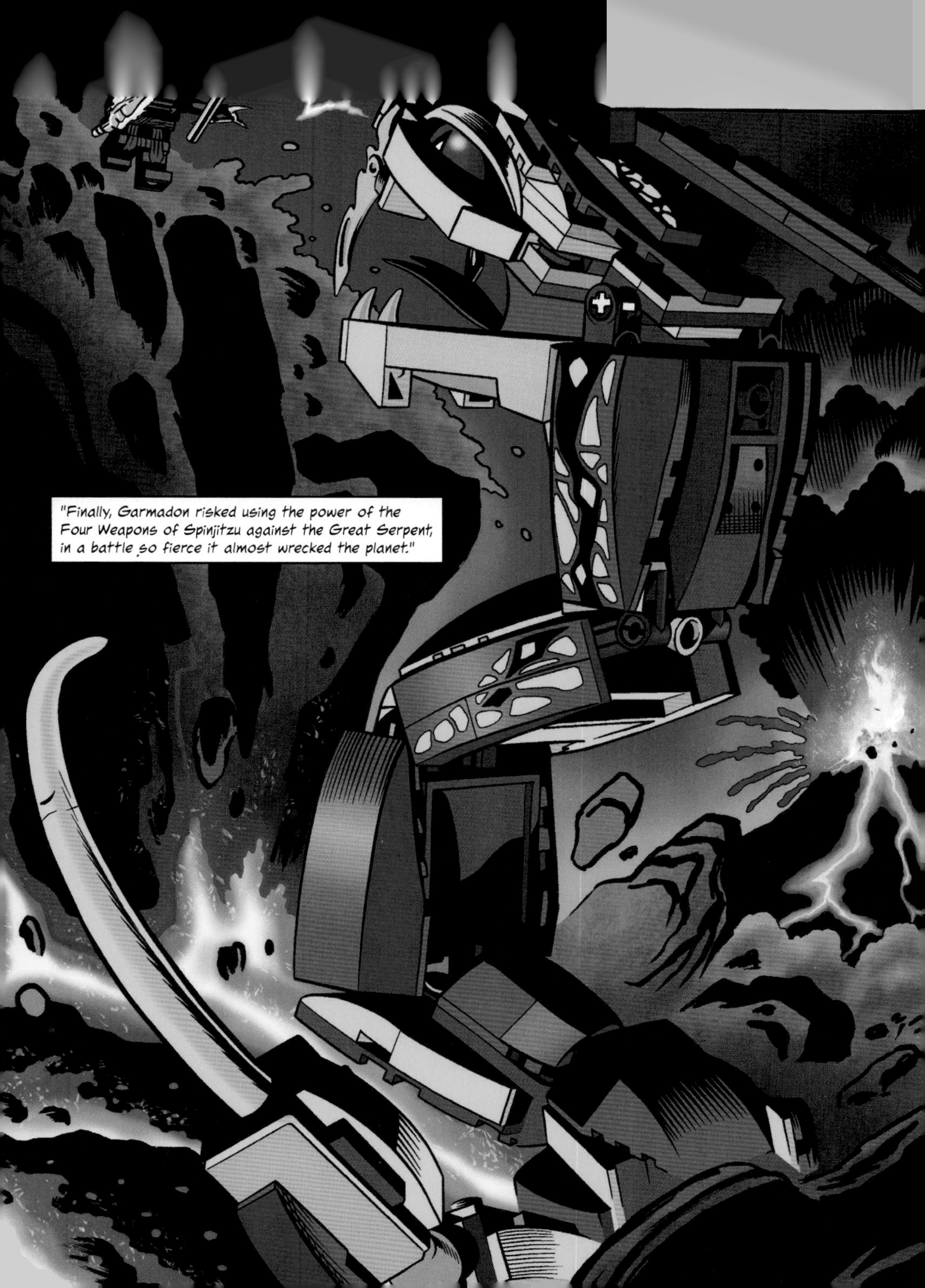
"Finally, Garmadon risked using the power of the Four Weapons of Spinjitzu against the Great Serpent, in a battle so fierce it almost wrecked the planet."

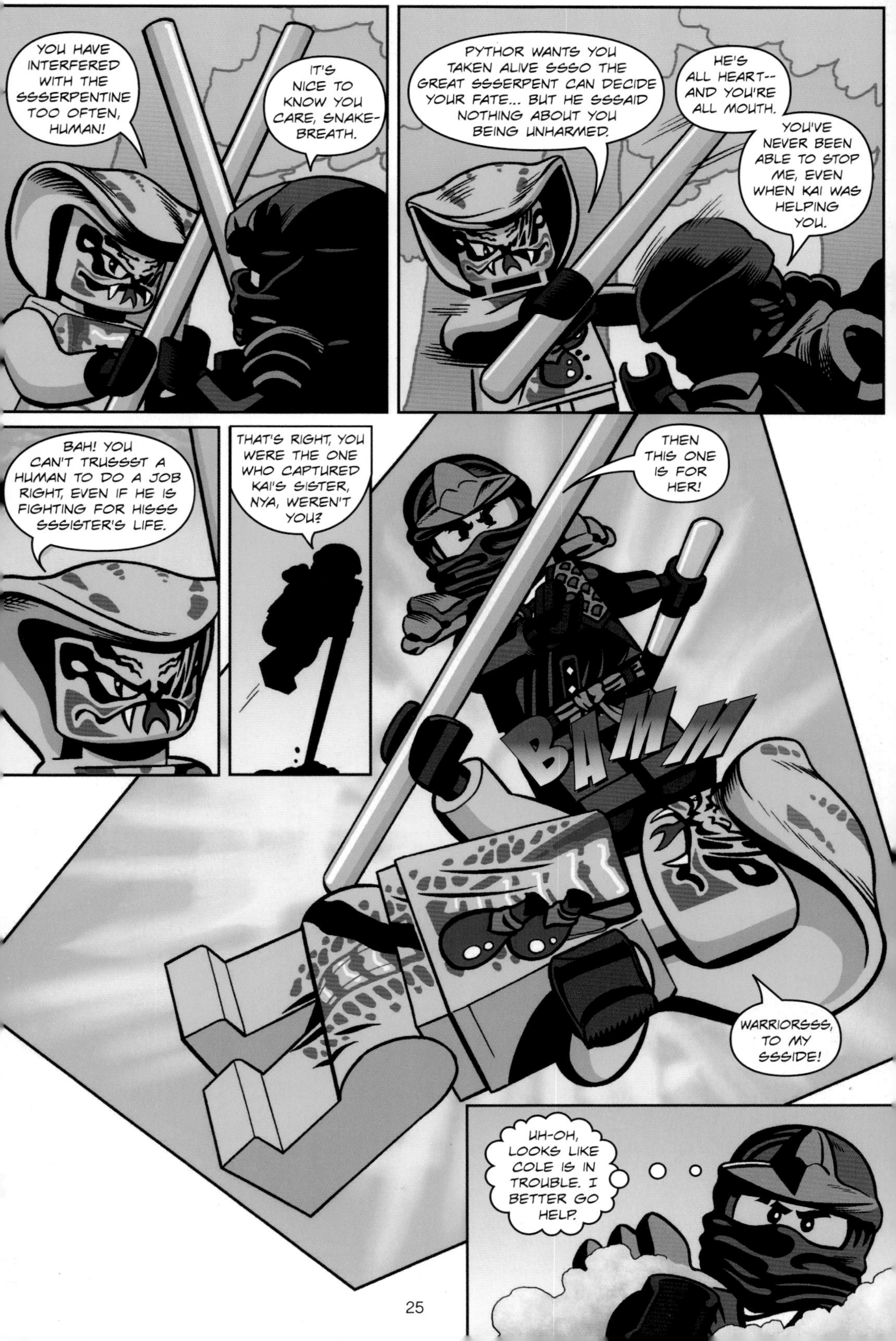

YOU HAVE INTERFERED WITH THE SSSERPENTINE TOO OFTEN, HUMAN!
IT'S NICE TO KNOW YOU CARE, SNAKE-BREATH.
PYTHOR WANTS YOU TAKEN ALIVE SSSO THE GREAT SSSERPENT CAN DECIDE YOUR FATE... BUT HE SSSAID NOTHING ABOUT YOU BEING UNHARMED.
HE'S ALL HEART-- AND YOU'RE ALL MOUTH.
YOU'VE NEVER BEEN ABLE TO STOP ME, EVEN WHEN KAI WAS HELPING YOU.
BAH! YOU CAN'T TRUSSST A HUMAN TO DO A JOB RIGHT, EVEN IF HE IS FIGHTING FOR HISSS SSSISTER'S LIFE.
THAT'S RIGHT, YOU WERE THE ONE WHO CAPTURED KAI'S SISTER, NYA, WEREN'T YOU?
THEN THIS ONE IS FOR HER!
BAMM
WARRIORSSS, TO MY SSSIDE!
UH-OH, LOOKS LIKE COLE IS IN TROUBLE. I BETTER GO HELP.

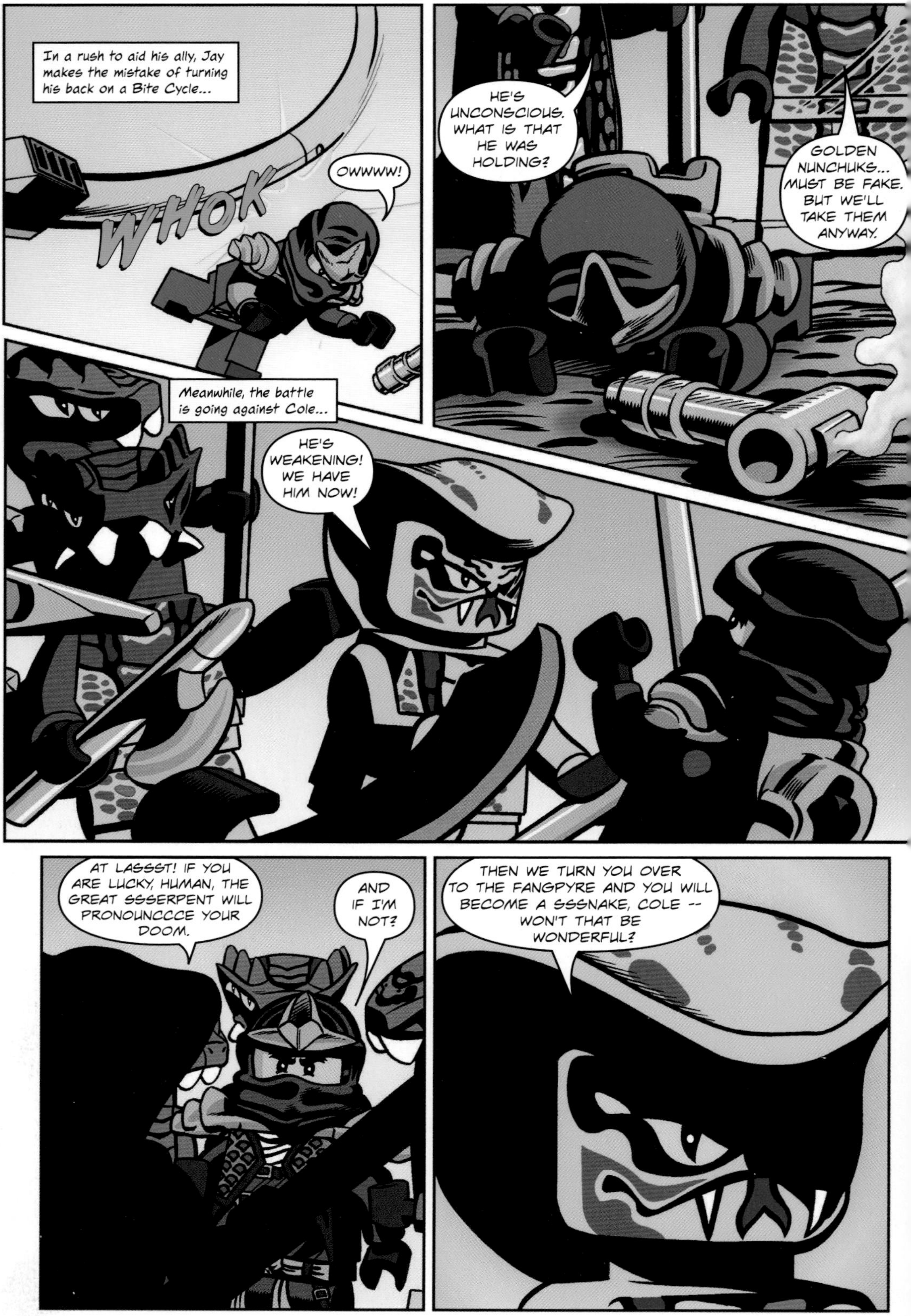

In a rush to aid his ally, Jay makes the mistake of turning his back on a Bite Cycle...
WHOK
OWWWW!
HE'S UNCONSCIOUS. WHAT IS THAT HE WAS HOLDING?
GOLDEN NUNCHUKS... MUST BE FAKE. BUT WE'LL TAKE THEM ANYWAY.
Meanwhile, the battle is going against Cole...
HE'S WEAKENING! WE HAVE HIM NOW!
AT LASSST! IF YOU ARE LUCKY, HUMAN, THE GREAT SSSERPENT WILL PRONOUNCCCE YOUR DOOM.
AND IF I'M NOT?
THEN WE TURN YOU OVER TO THE FANGPYRE AND YOU WILL BECOME A SSSNAKE, COLE -- WON'T THAT BE WONDERFUL?

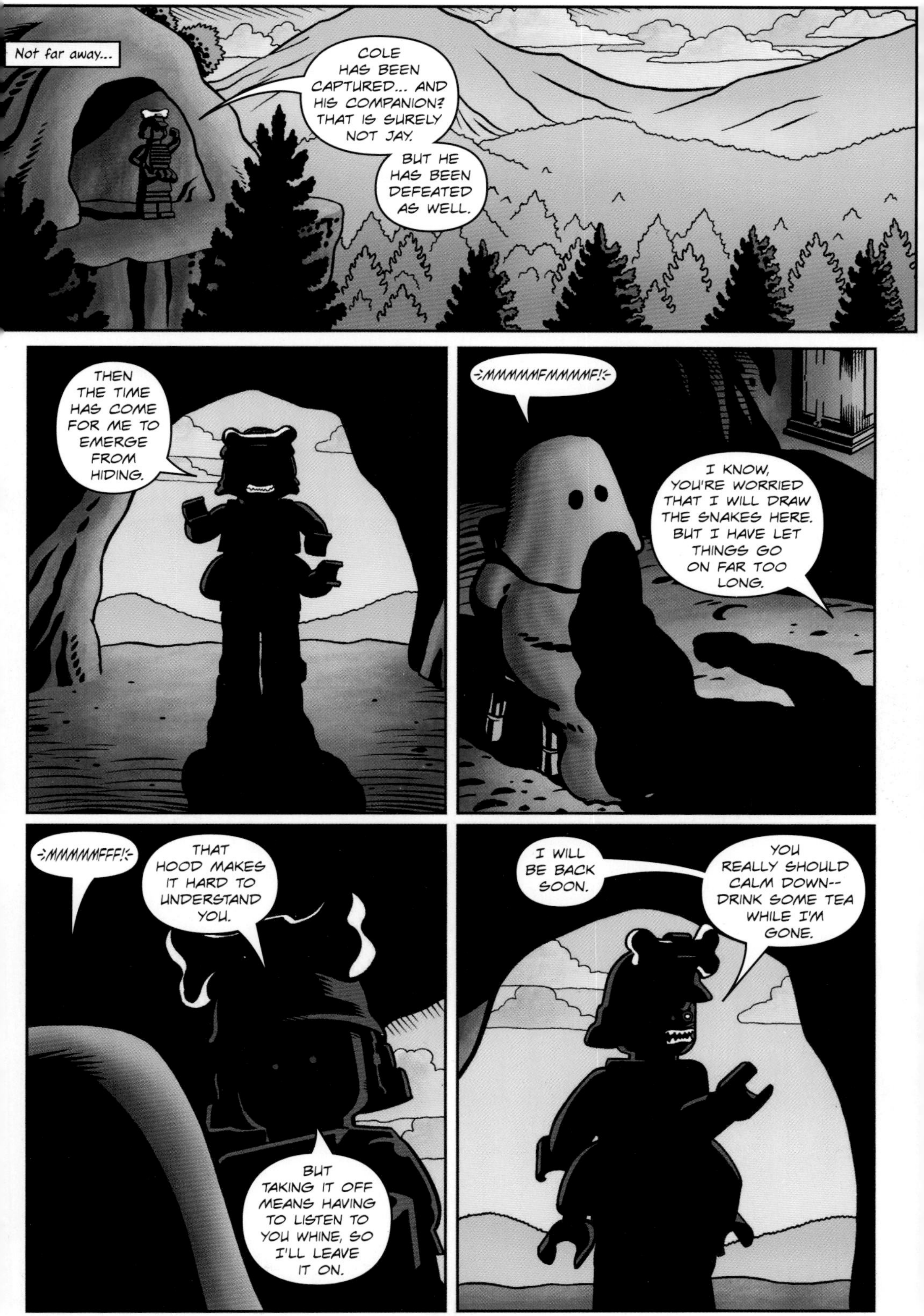
Not far away...
COLE HAS BEEN CAPTURED... AND HIS COMPANION? THAT IS SURELY NOT JAY.
BUT HE HAS BEEN DEFEATED AS WELL.
THEN THE TIME HAS COME FOR ME TO EMERGE FROM HIDING.
-MMMMMFMMMMF!-
I KNOW, YOU'RE WORRIED THAT I WILL DRAW THE SNAKES HERE. BUT I HAVE LET THINGS GO ON FAR TOO LONG.
-MMMMMFFF!-
THAT HOOD MAKES IT HARD TO UNDERSTAND YOU.
BUT TAKING IT OFF MEANS HAVING TO LISTEN TO YOU WHINE, SO I'LL LEAVE IT ON.
I WILL BE BACK SOON.
YOU REALLY SHOULD CALM DOWN-- DRINK SOME TEA WHILE I'M GONE.

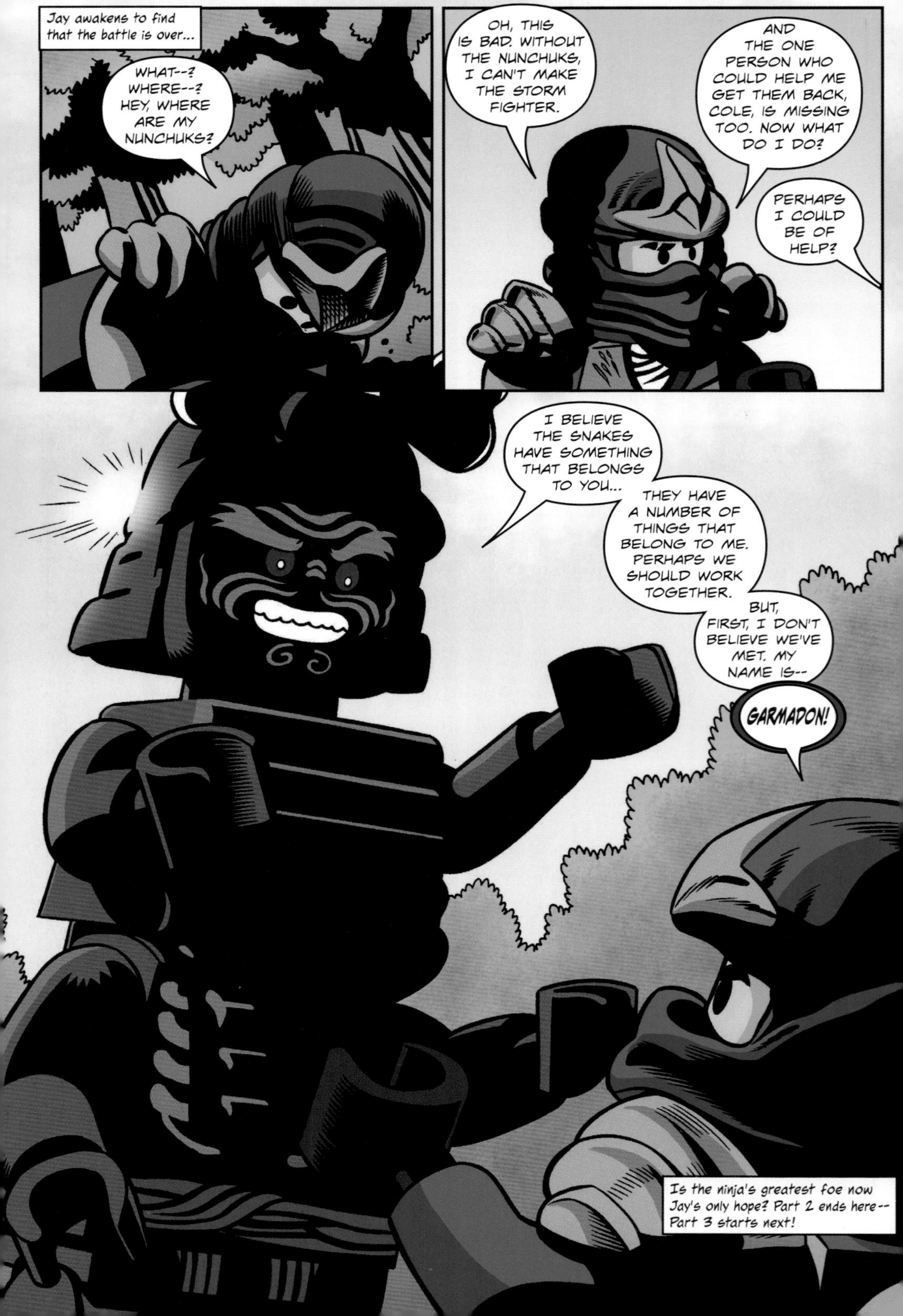
Jay awakens to find that the battle is over...
WHAT--? WHERE--? HEY, WHERE ARE MY NUNCHUKS?
OH, THIS IS BAD. WITHOUT THE NUNCHUKS, I CAN'T MAKE THE STORM FIGHTER.
AND THE ONE PERSON WHO COULD HELP ME GET THEM BACK, COLE, IS MISSING TOO. NOW WHAT DO I DO?
PERHAPS I COULD BE OF HELP?
I BELIEVE THE SNAKES HAVE SOMETHING THAT BELONGS TO YOU...
THEY HAVE A NUMBER OF THINGS THAT BELONG TO ME. PERHAPS WE SHOULD WORK TOGETHER.
BUT, FIRST, I DON'T BELIEVE WE'VE MET. MY NAME IS--
GARMADON!
Is the ninja's greatest foe now Jay's only hope? Part 2 ends here-- Part 3 starts next!

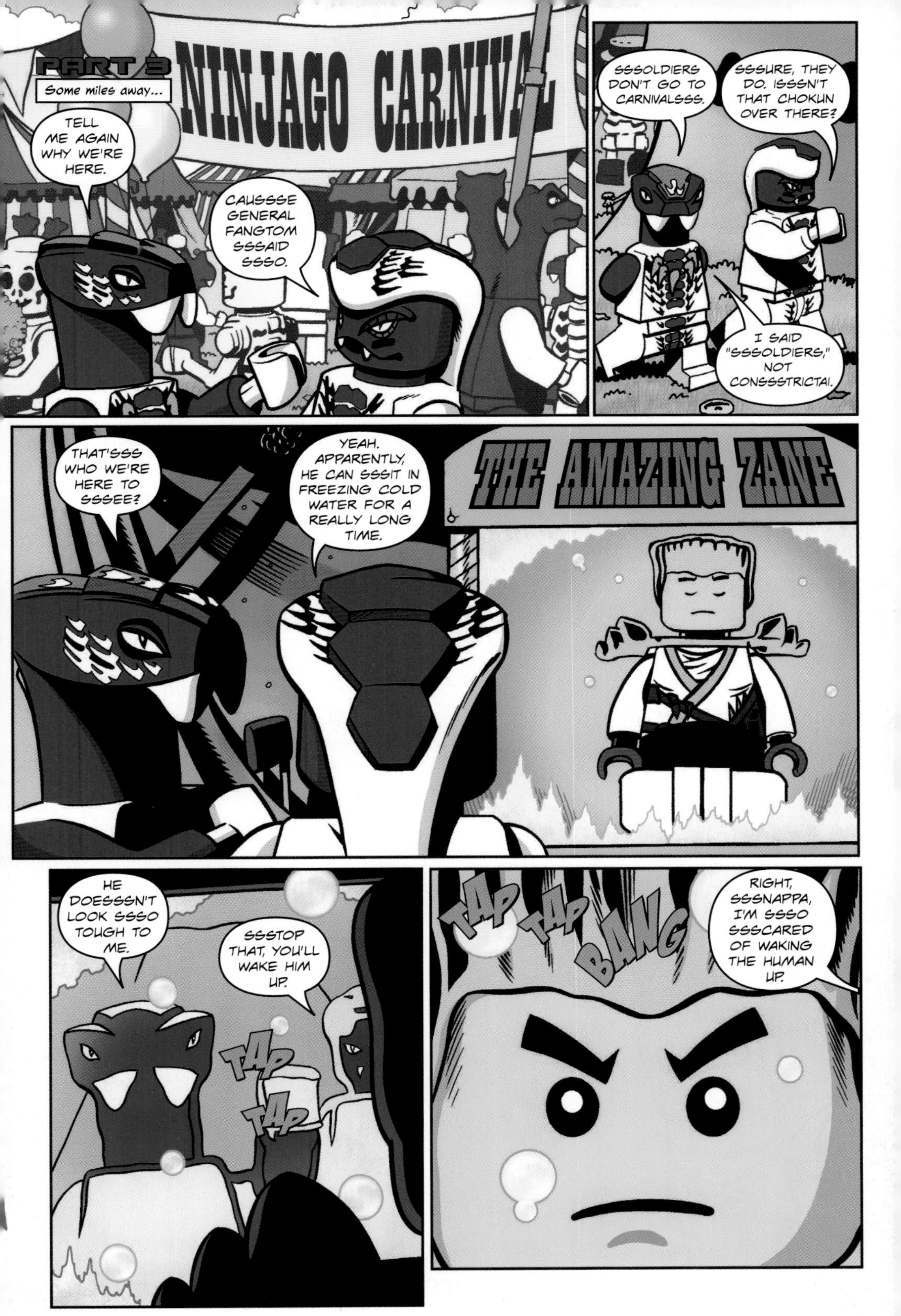

PART 3
Some miles away...
NINJAGO CARNIVAL
TELL ME AGAIN WHY WE'RE HERE.
CAUSSSE GENERAL FANGTOM SSSAID SSSO.
SSSOLDIERS DON'T GO TO CARNIVALSSS.
SSSURE, THEY DO. ISSSN'T THAT CHOKUN OVER THERE?
I SAID "SSSOLDIERS," NOT CONSSSTRICTAI.
THE AMAZING ZANE
THAT'SSS WHO WE'RE HERE TO SSSEE?
YEAH. APPARENTLY, HE CAN SSSIT IN FREEZING COLD WATER FOR A REALLY LONG TIME.
HE DOESSSN'T LOOK SSSO TOUGH TO ME.
SSSTOP THAT, YOU'LL WAKE HIM UP.
TAP
TAP
TAP
TAP
BANG
RIGHT, SSSNAPPA, I'M SSSO SSSCARED OF WAKING THE HUMAN UP.

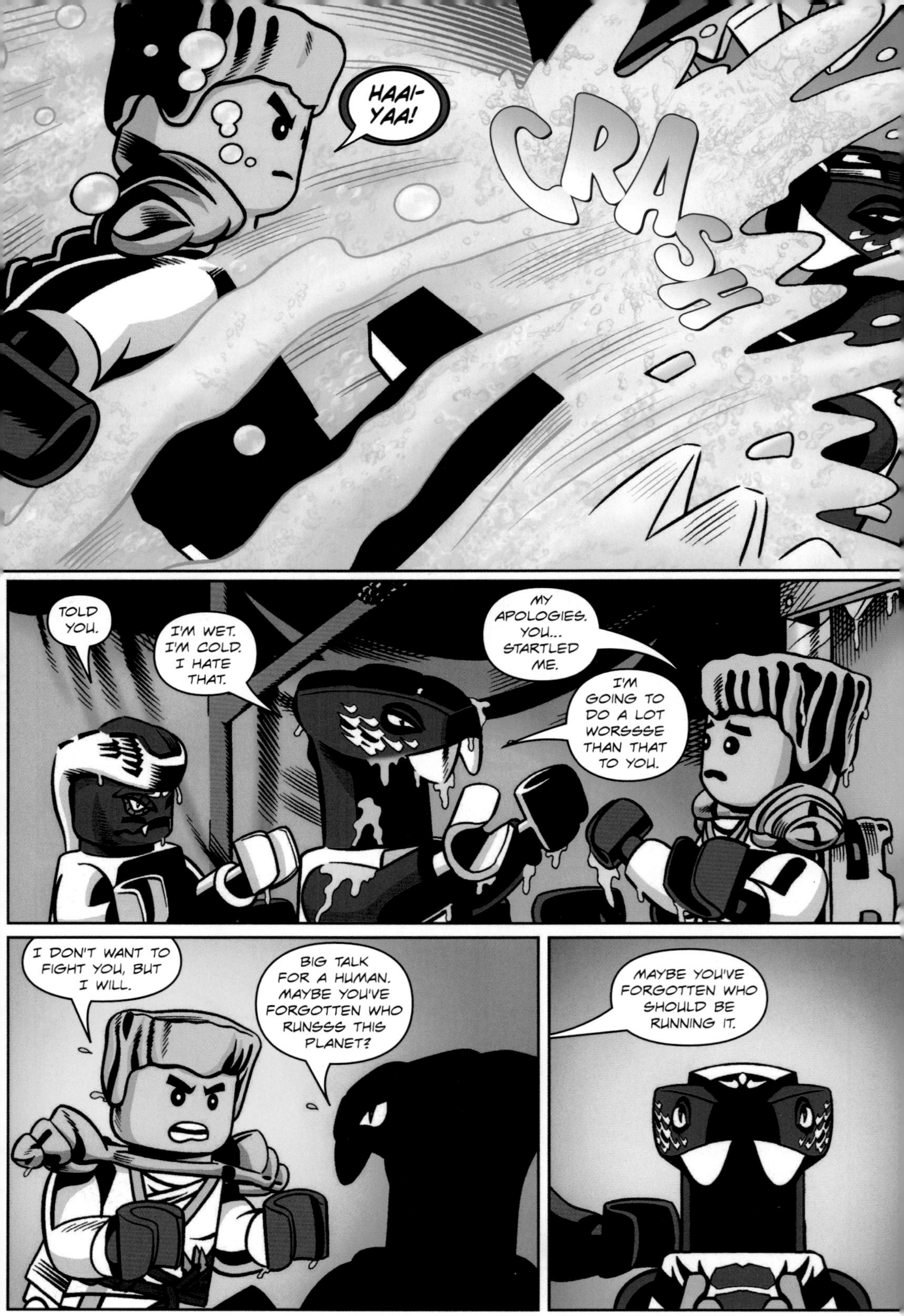
HAAI-YAA!
CRASH
TOLD YOU.
I'M WET. I'M COLD. I HATE THAT.
MY APOLOGIES. YOU... STARTLED ME.
I'M GOING TO DO A LOT WORSSSE THAN THAT TO YOU.
I DON'T WANT TO FIGHT YOU, BUT I WILL.
BIG TALK FOR A HUMAN. MAYBE YOU'VE FORGOTTEN WHO RUNSSS THIS PLANET?
MAYBE YOU'VE FORGOTTEN WHO SHOULD BE RUNNING IT.

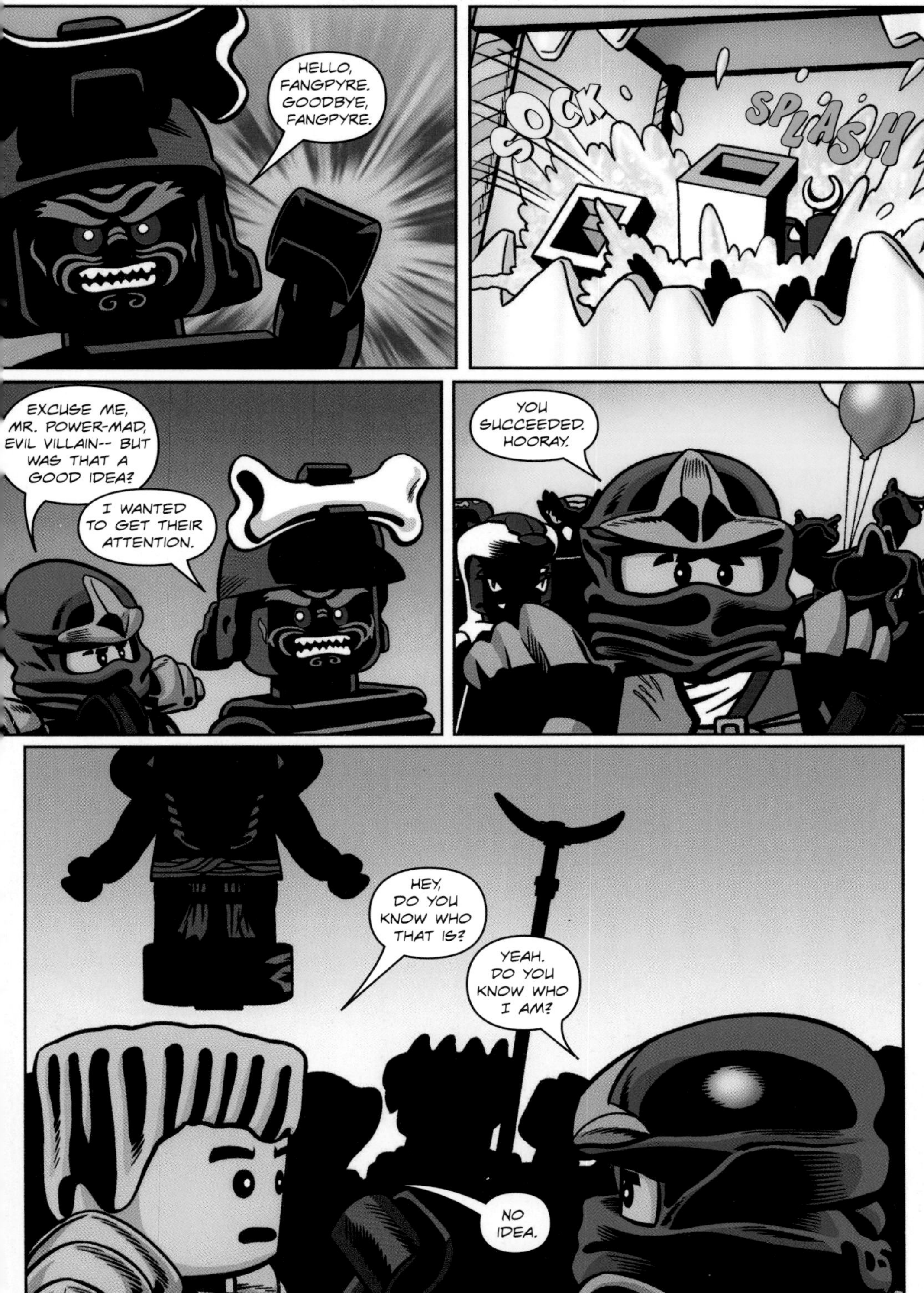
HELLO, FANGPYRE. GOODBYE, FANGPYRE.
SOCK
SPLASH
EXCUSE ME, MR. POWER-MAD, EVIL VILLAIN-- BUT WAS THAT A GOOD IDEA?
I WANTED TO GET THEIR ATTENTION.
YOU SUCCEEDED. HOORAY.
HEY, DO YOU KNOW WHO THAT IS?
YEAH. DO YOU KNOW WHO I AM?
NO IDEA.

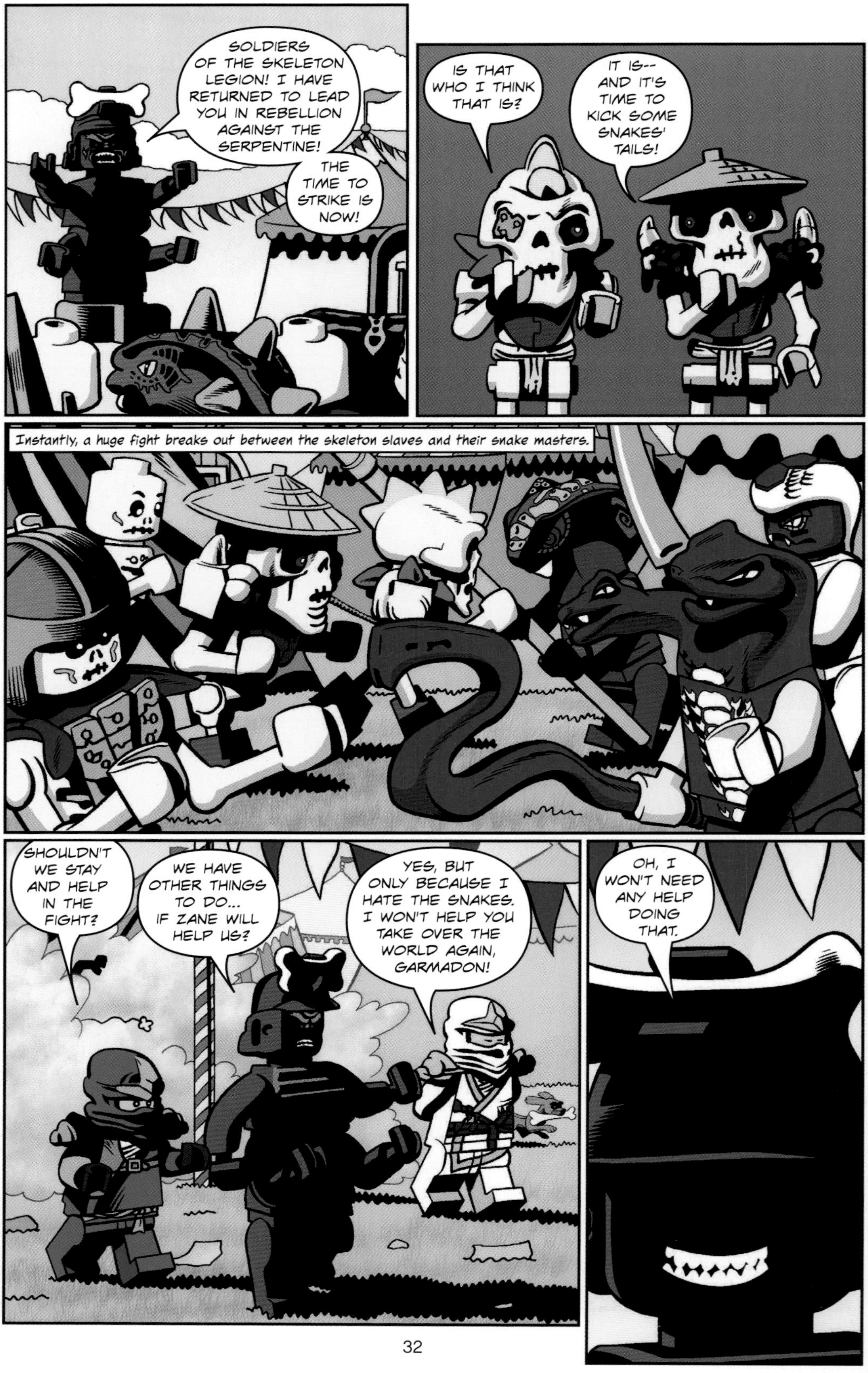
SOLDIERS OF THE SKELETON LEGION! I HAVE RETURNED TO LEAD YOU IN REBELLION AGAINST THE SERPENTINE!
THE TIME TO STRIKE IS NOW!
IS THAT WHO I THINK THAT IS?
IT IS-- AND IT'S TIME TO KICK SOME SNAKES' TAILS!
Instantly, a huge fight breaks out between the skeleton slaves and their snake masters.
SHOULDN'T WE STAY AND HELP IN THE FIGHT?
WE HAVE OTHER THINGS TO DO... IF ZANE WILL HELP US?
YES, BUT ONLY BECAUSE I HATE THE SNAKES. I WON'T HELP YOU TAKE OVER THE WORLD AGAIN, GARMADON!
OH, I WON'T NEED ANY HELP DOING THAT.

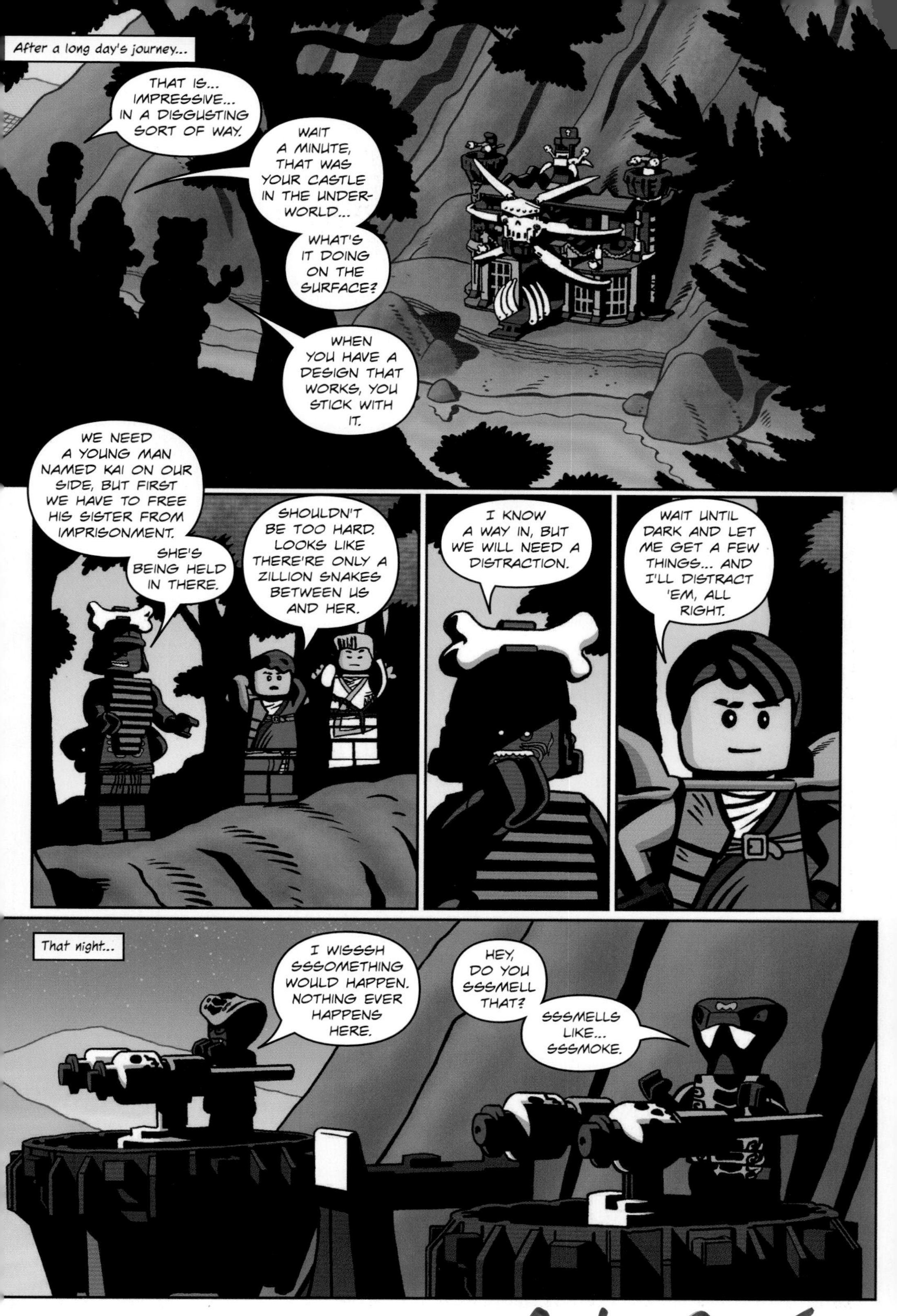
After a long day's journey...
THAT IS... IMPRESSIVE... IN A DISGUSTING SORT OF WAY.
WAIT A MINUTE, THAT WAS YOUR CASTLE IN THE UNDER-WORLD...
WHAT'S IT DOING ON THE SURFACE?
WHEN YOU HAVE A DESIGN THAT WORKS, YOU STICK WITH IT.
WE NEED A YOUNG MAN NAMED KAI ON OUR SIDE, BUT FIRST WE HAVE TO FREE HIS SISTER FROM IMPRISONMENT.
SHE'S BEING HELD IN THERE.
SHOULDN'T BE TOO HARD. LOOKS LIKE THERE'RE ONLY A ZILLION SNAKES BETWEEN US AND HER.
I KNOW A WAY IN, BUT WE WILL NEED A DISTRACTION.
WAIT UNTIL DARK AND LET ME GET A FEW THINGS... AND I'LL DISTRACT 'EM, ALL RIGHT.
That night...
I WISSSH SSSOMETHING WOULD HAPPEN. NOTHING EVER HAPPENS HERE.
HEY, DO YOU SSSMELL THAT?
SSSMELLS LIKE... SSSMOKE.

Ruben Gines

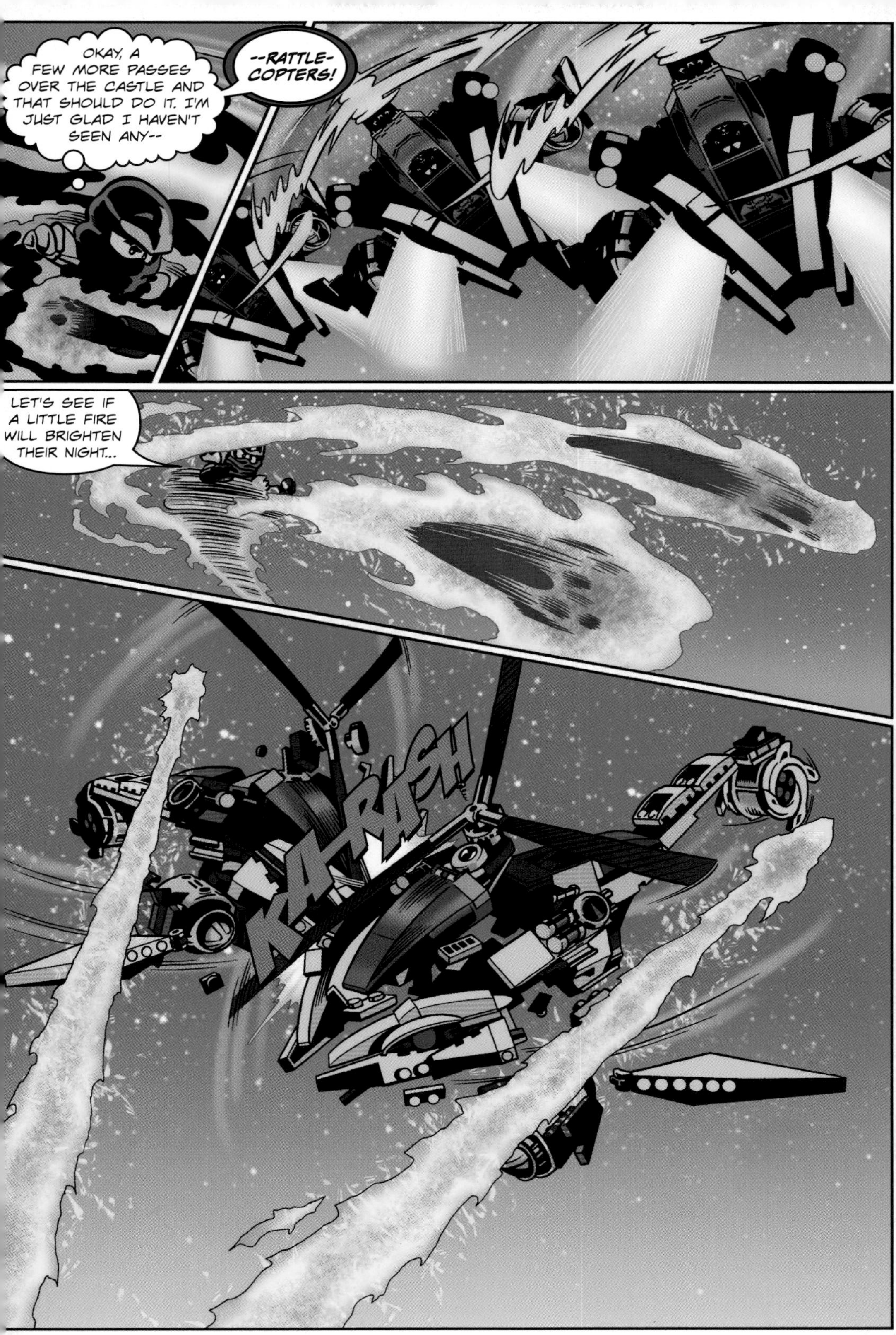
OKAY, A FEW MORE PASSES OVER THE CASTLE AND THAT SHOULD DO IT. I'M JUST GLAD I HAVEN'T SEEN ANY--
--RATTLE-COPTERS!
LET'S SEE IF A LITTLE FIRE WILL BRIGHTEN THEIR NIGHT...
KA-RASH

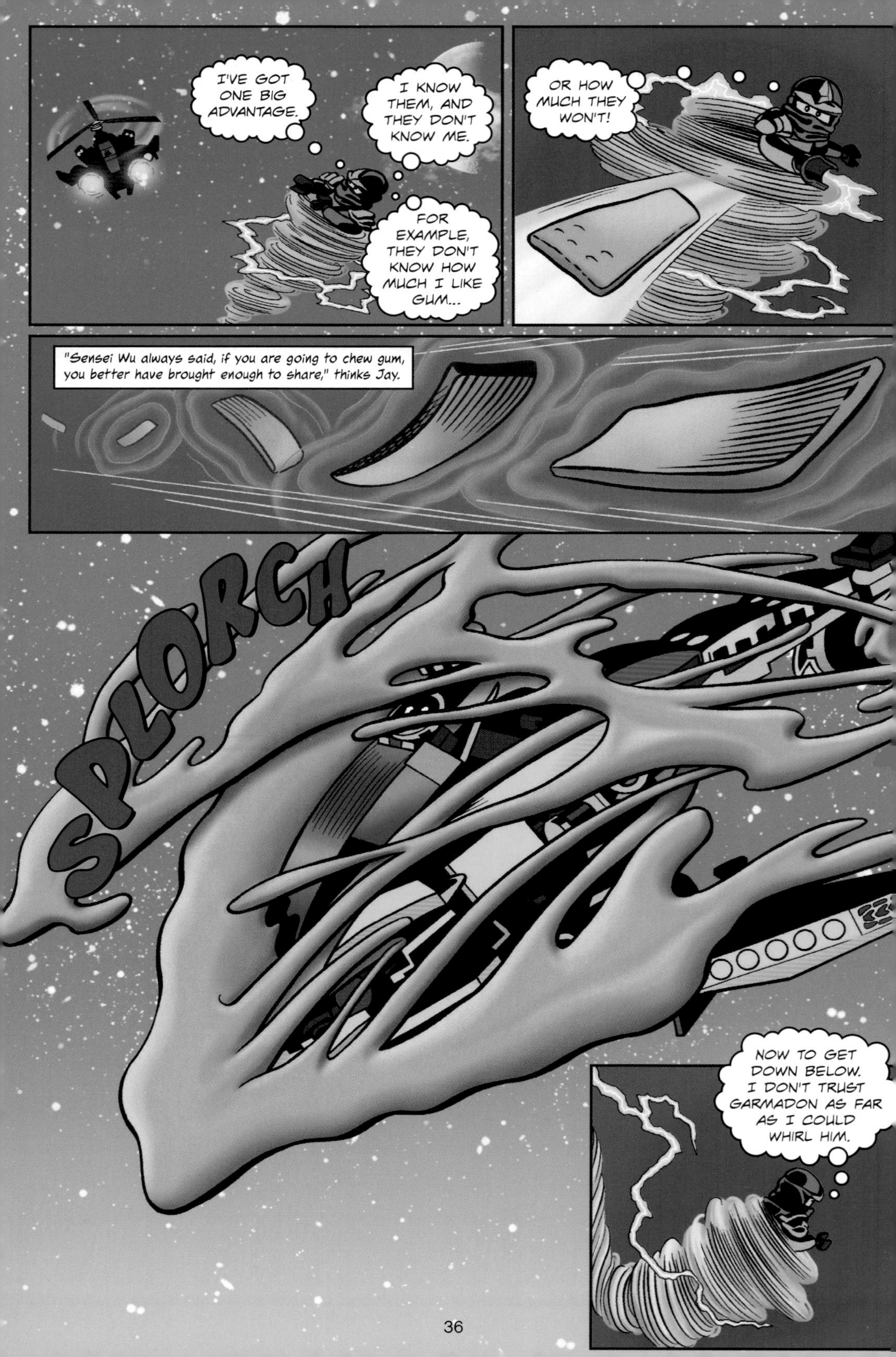
I'VE GOT ONE BIG ADVANTAGE.
I KNOW THEM, AND THEY DON'T KNOW ME.
FOR EXAMPLE, THEY DON'T KNOW HOW MUCH I LIKE GUM...
OR HOW MUCH THEY WON'T!
"Sensei Wu always said, if you are going to chew gum, you better have brought enough to share," thinks Jay.
SPLORCH
NOW TO GET DOWN BELOW. I DON'T TRUST GARMADON AS FAR AS I COULD WHIRL HIM.

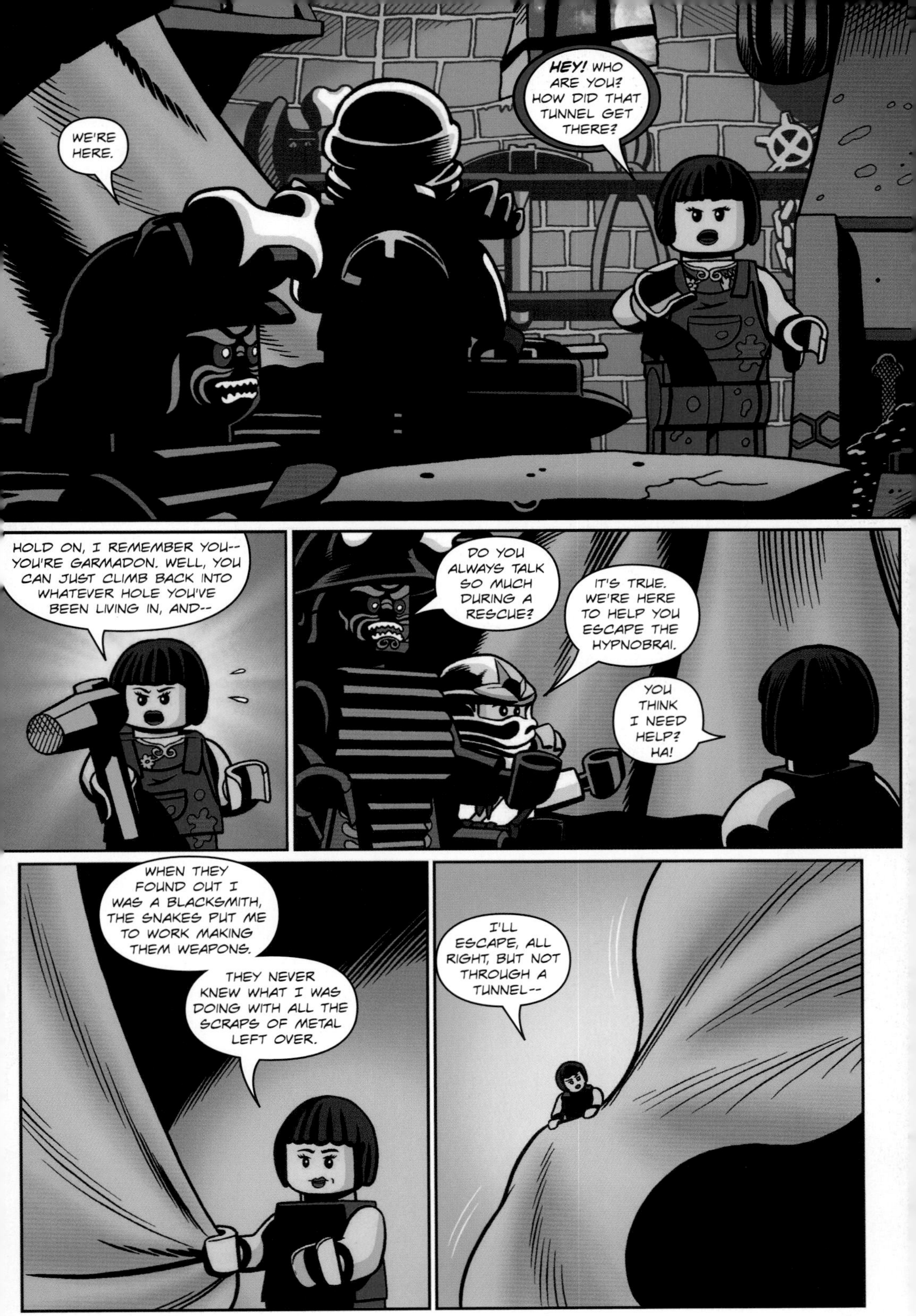
WE'RE HERE.
HEY! WHO ARE YOU? HOW DID THAT TUNNEL GET THERE?
HOLD ON, I REMEMBER YOU-- YOU'RE GARMADON. WELL, YOU CAN JUST CLIMB BACK INTO WHATEVER HOLE YOU'VE BEEN LIVING IN, AND--
DO YOU ALWAYS TALK SO MUCH DURING A RESCUE?
IT'S TRUE. WE'RE HERE TO HELP YOU ESCAPE THE HYPNOBRAI.
YOU THINK I NEED HELP? HA!
WHEN THEY FOUND OUT I WAS A BLACKSMITH, THE SNAKES PUT ME TO WORK MAKING THEM WEAPONS.
THEY NEVER KNEW WHAT I WAS DOING WITH ALL THE SCRAPS OF METAL LEFT OVER.
I'LL ESCAPE, ALL RIGHT, BUT NOT THROUGH A TUNNEL--

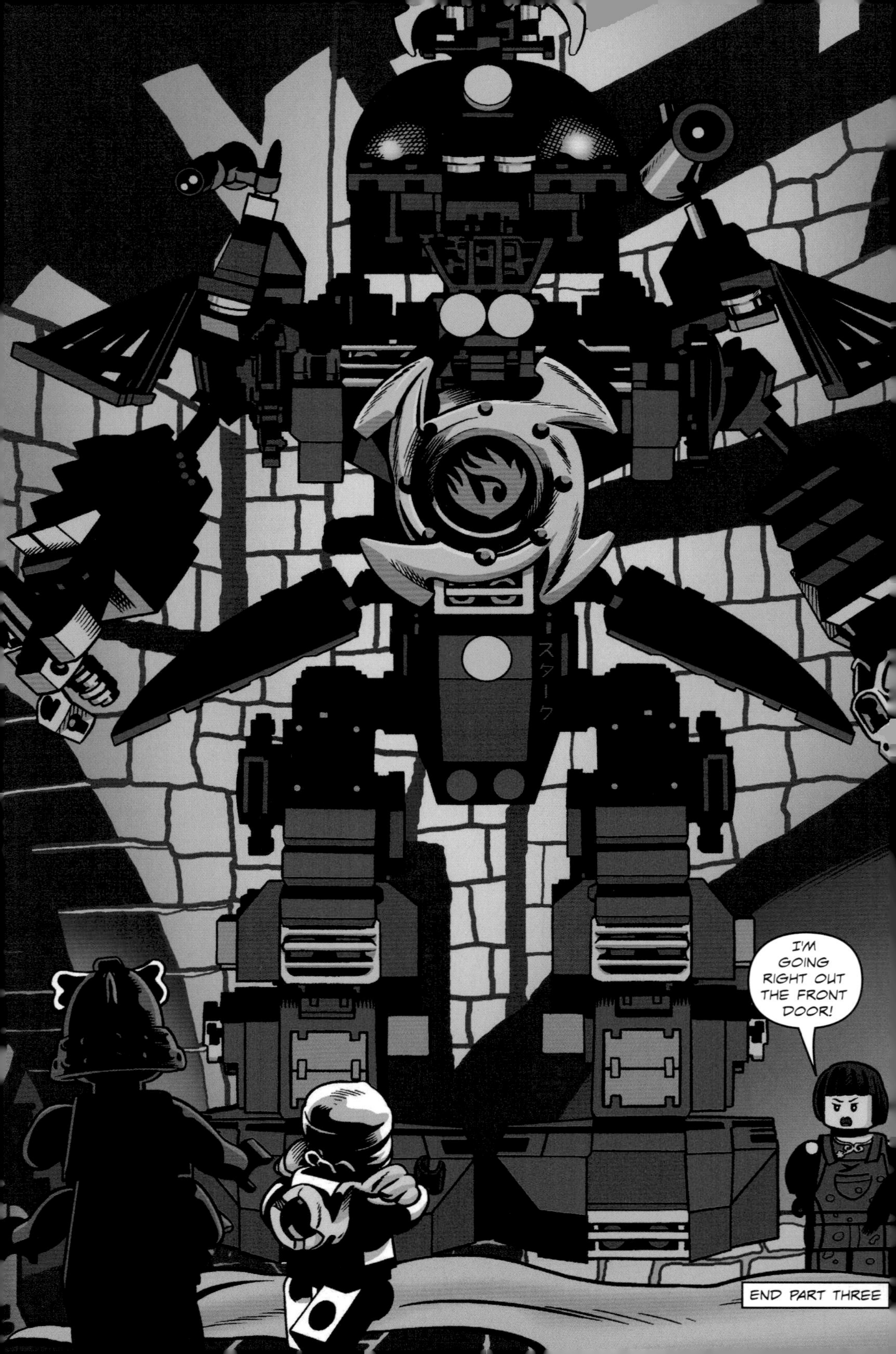
スターク
I'M GOING RIGHT OUT THE FRONT DOOR!
END PART THREE

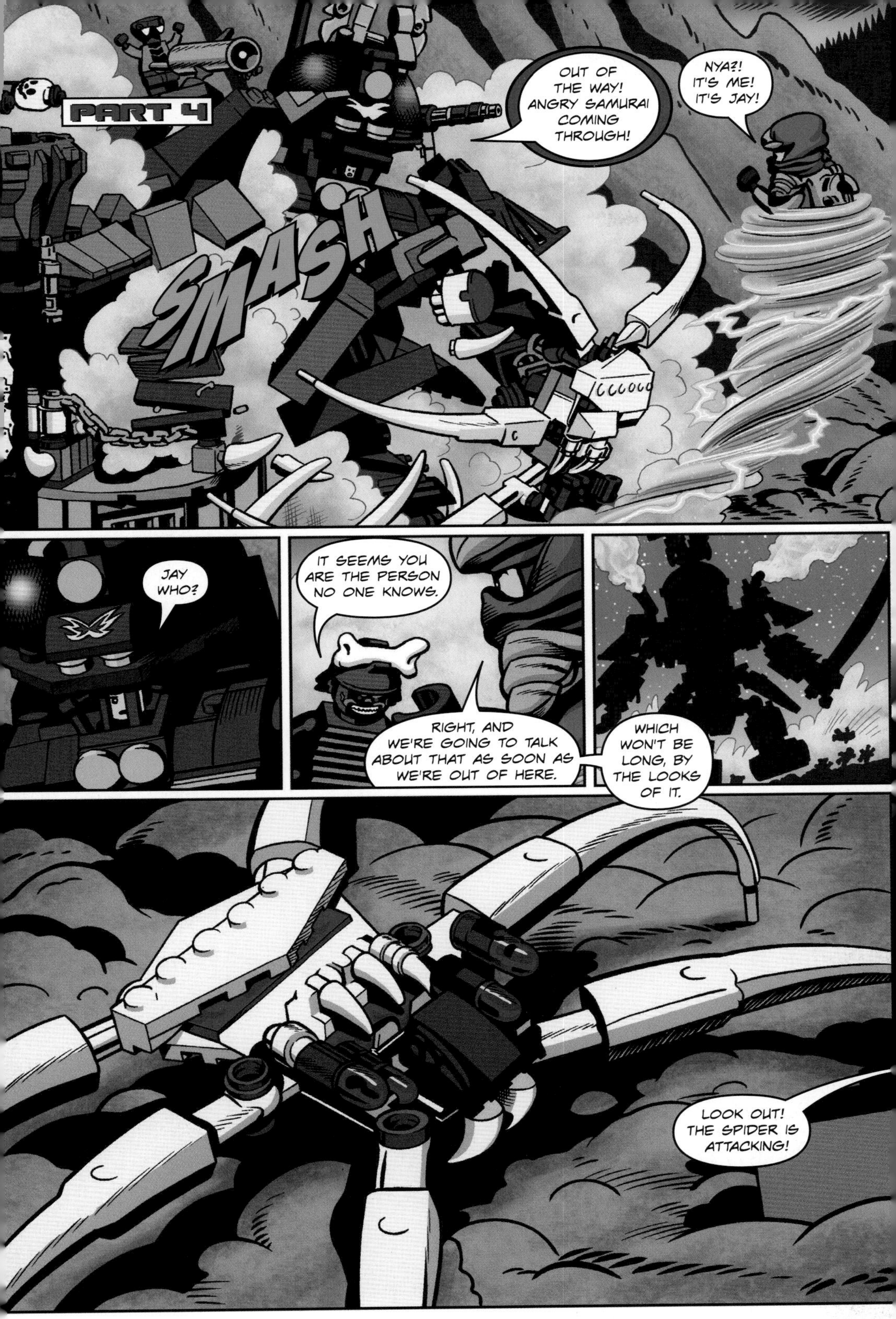
PART 4
SMASH
OUT OF THE WAY! ANGRY SAMURAI COMING THROUGH!
NYA?! IT'S ME! IT'S JAY!
JAY WHO?
IT SEEMS YOU ARE THE PERSON NO ONE KNOWS.
RIGHT, AND WE'RE GOING TO TALK ABOUT THAT AS SOON AS WE'RE OUT OF HERE.
WHICH WON'T BE LONG, BY THE LOOKS OF IT.
LOOK OUT! THE SPIDER IS ATTACKING!

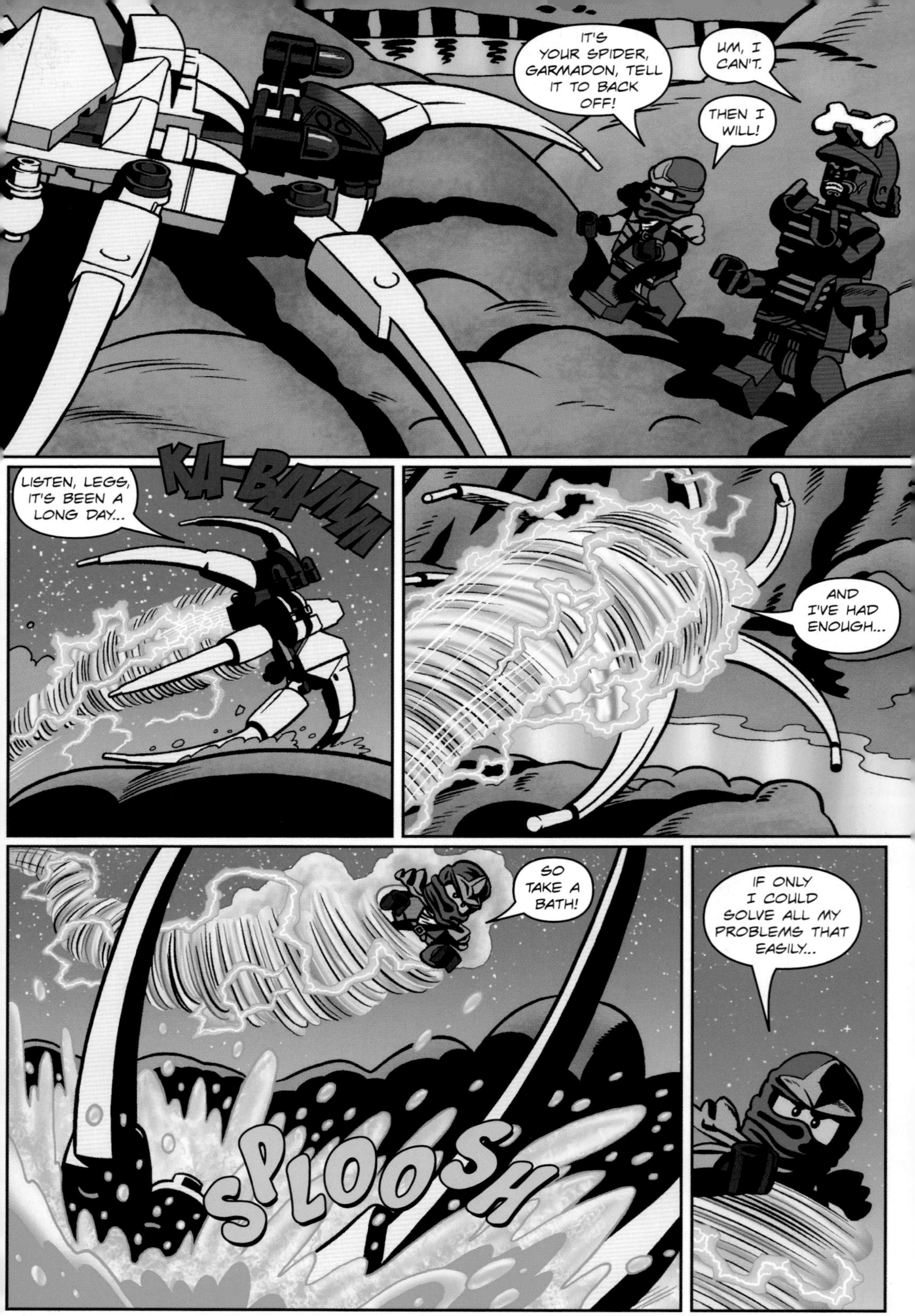
IT'S YOUR SPIDER, GARMADON, TELL IT TO BACK OFF!
UM, I CAN'T.
THEN I WILL!
KA-BAMMM
LISTEN, LEGS, IT'S BEEN A LONG DAY...
AND I'VE HAD ENOUGH...
SO TAKE A BATH!
SPLOOSH
IF ONLY I COULD SOLVE ALL MY PROBLEMS THAT EASILY...

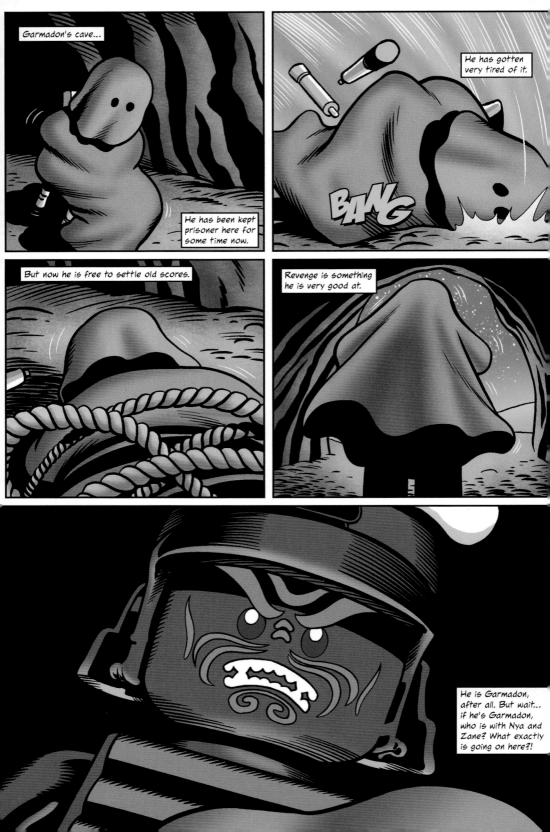

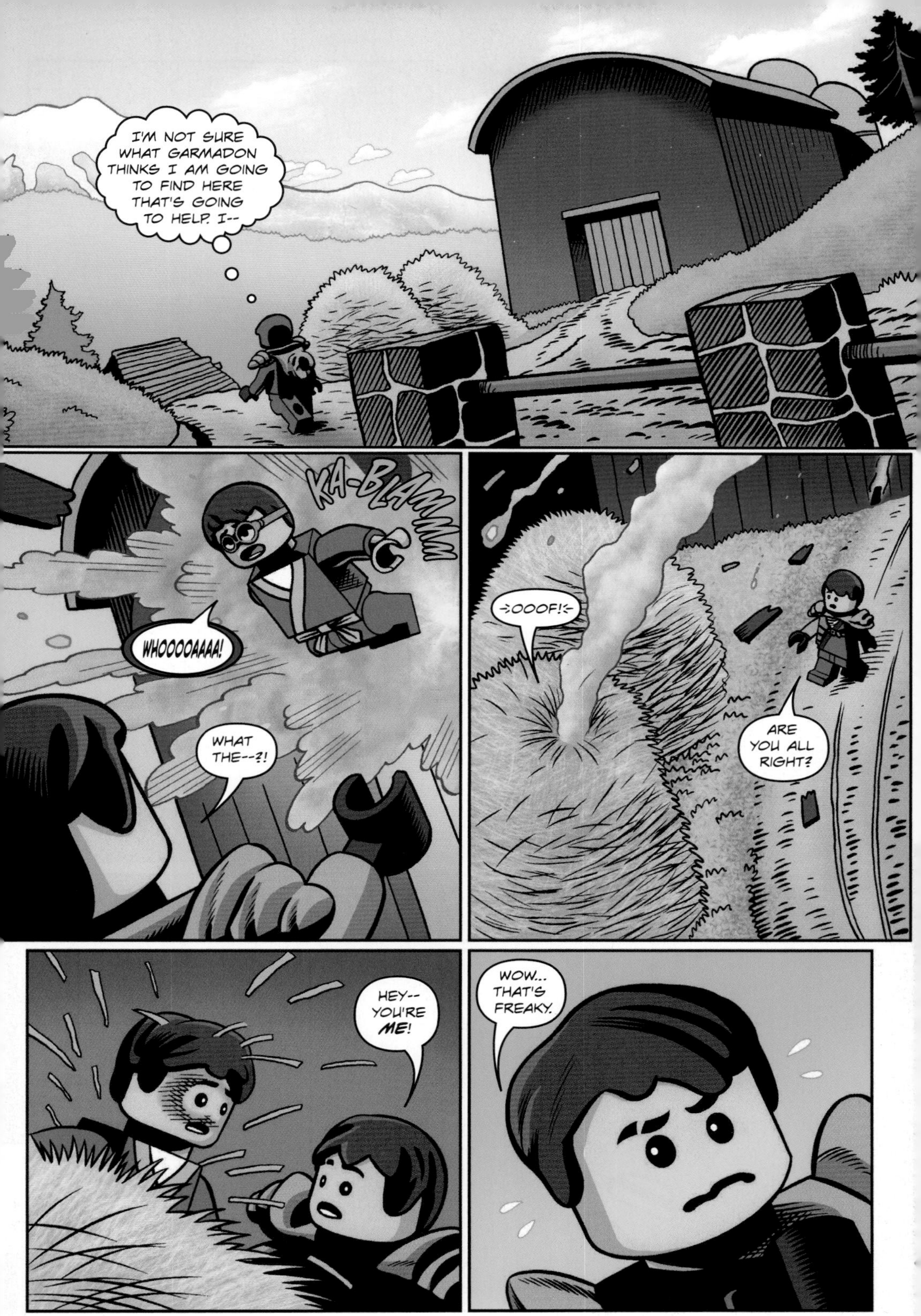
I'M NOT SURE WHAT GARMADON THINKS I AM GOING TO FIND HERE THAT'S GOING TO HELP. I--
KA-BLAMMM
WHOOOOAAAA!
WHAT THE--?!
OOOF!
ARE YOU ALL RIGHT?
HEY-- YOU'RE ME!
WOW... THAT'S FREAKY.

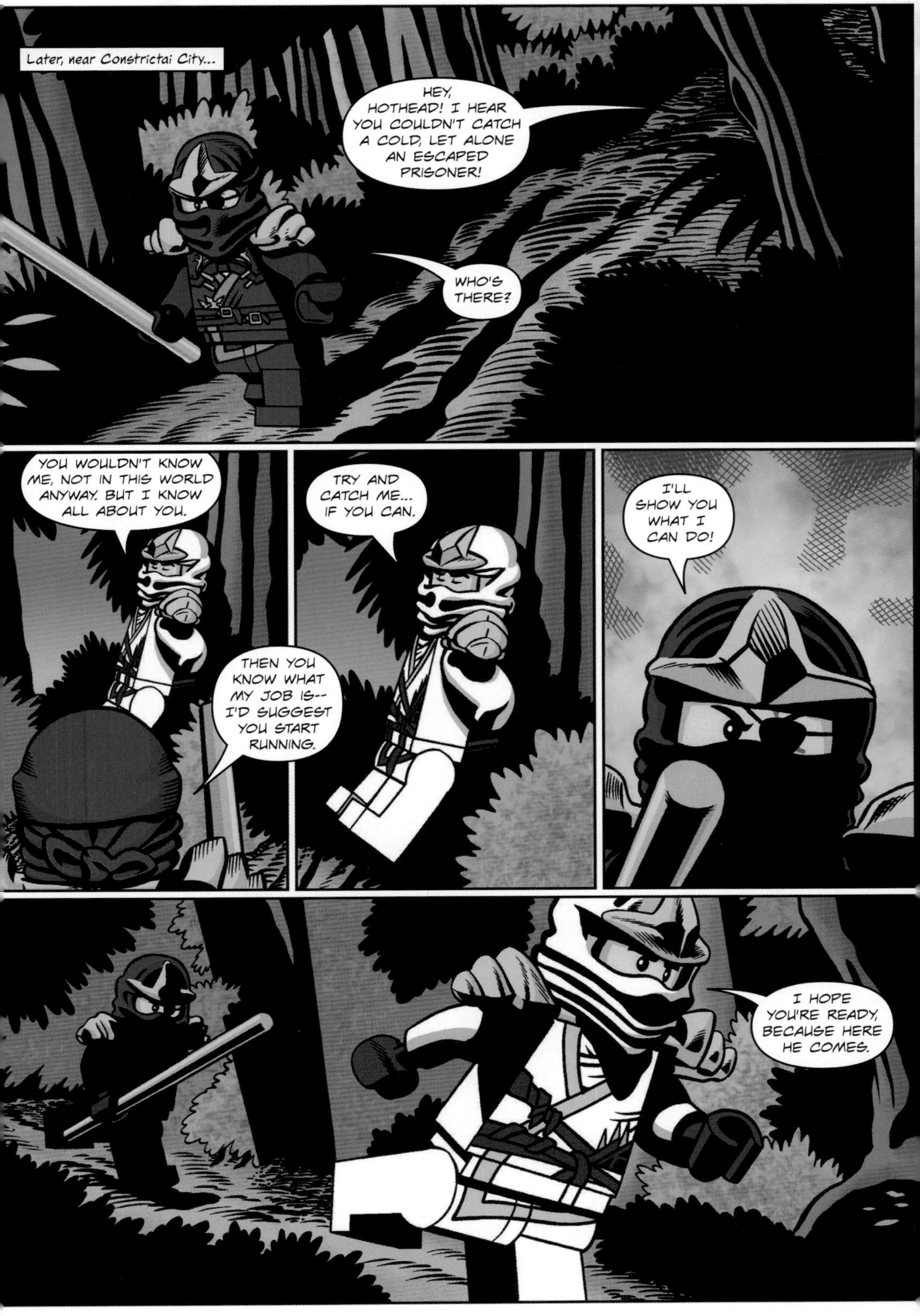
Later, near Constrictai City...
HEY, HOTHEAD! I HEAR YOU COULDN'T CATCH A COLD, LET ALONE AN ESCAPED PRISONER!
WHO'S THERE?
YOU WOULDN'T KNOW ME, NOT IN THIS WORLD ANYWAY. BUT I KNOW ALL ABOUT YOU.
THEN YOU KNOW WHAT MY JOB IS-- I'D SUGGEST YOU START RUNNING.
TRY AND CATCH ME... IF YOU CAN.
I'LL SHOW YOU WHAT I CAN DO!
I HOPE YOU'RE READY, BECAUSE HERE HE COMES.

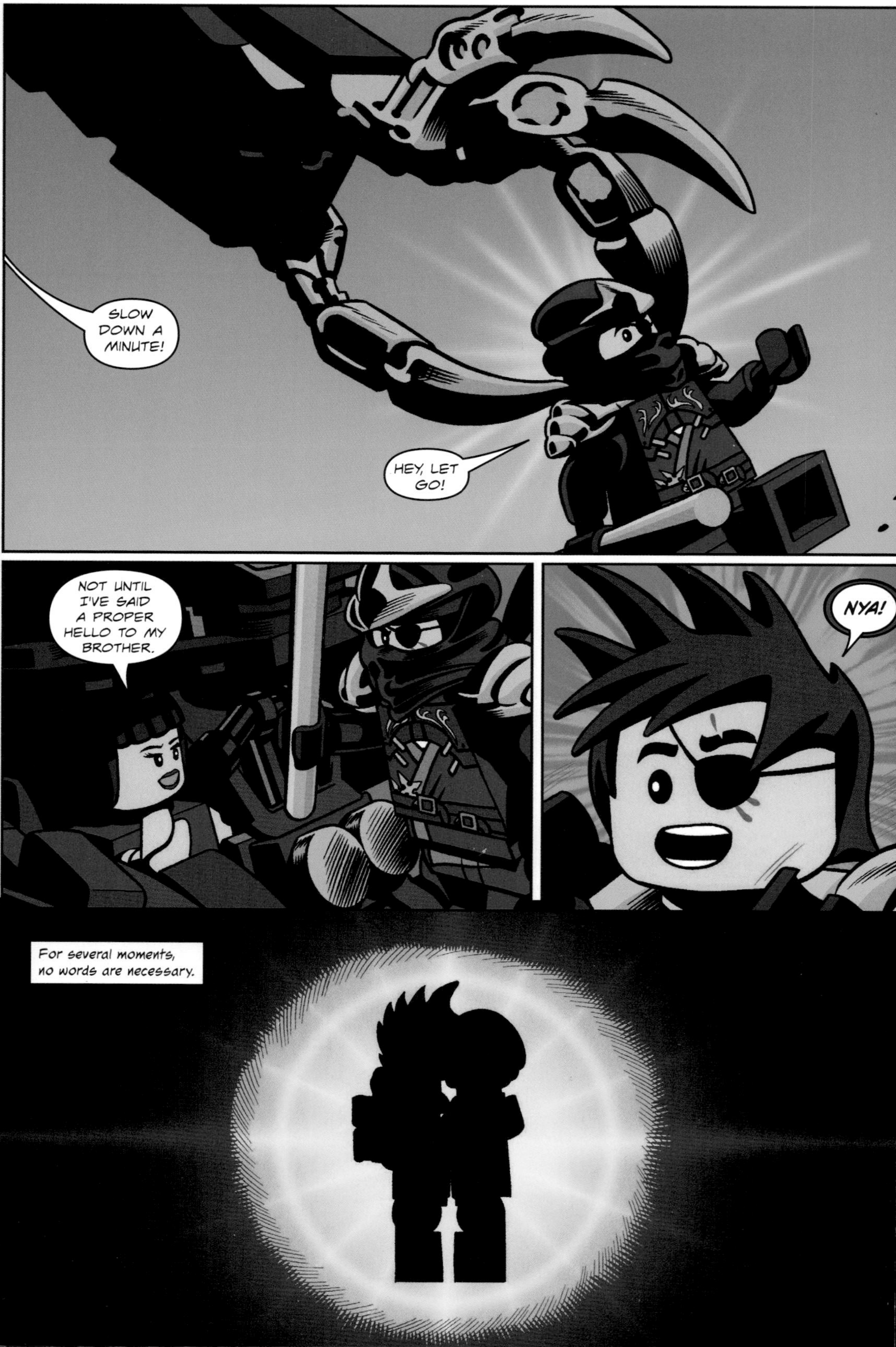
SLOW DOWN A MINUTE!
HEY, LET GO!
NOT UNTIL I'VE SAID A PROPER HELLO TO MY BROTHER.
NYA!
For several moments, no words are necessary.

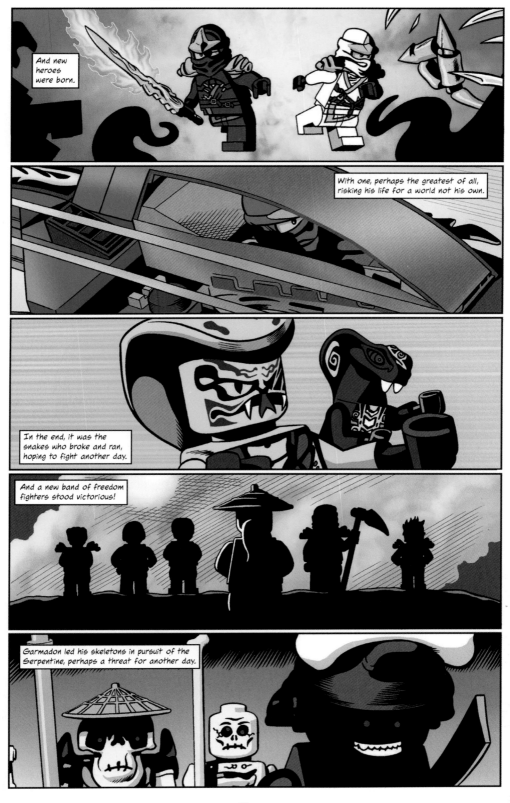

PART 5

And new heroes were born.

With one, perhaps the greatest of all, risking his life for a world not his own.

In the end, it was the snakes who broke and ran, hoping to fight another day.

And a new band of freedom fighters stood victorious!

Garmadon led his skeletons in pursuit of the Serpentine, perhaps a threat for another day.

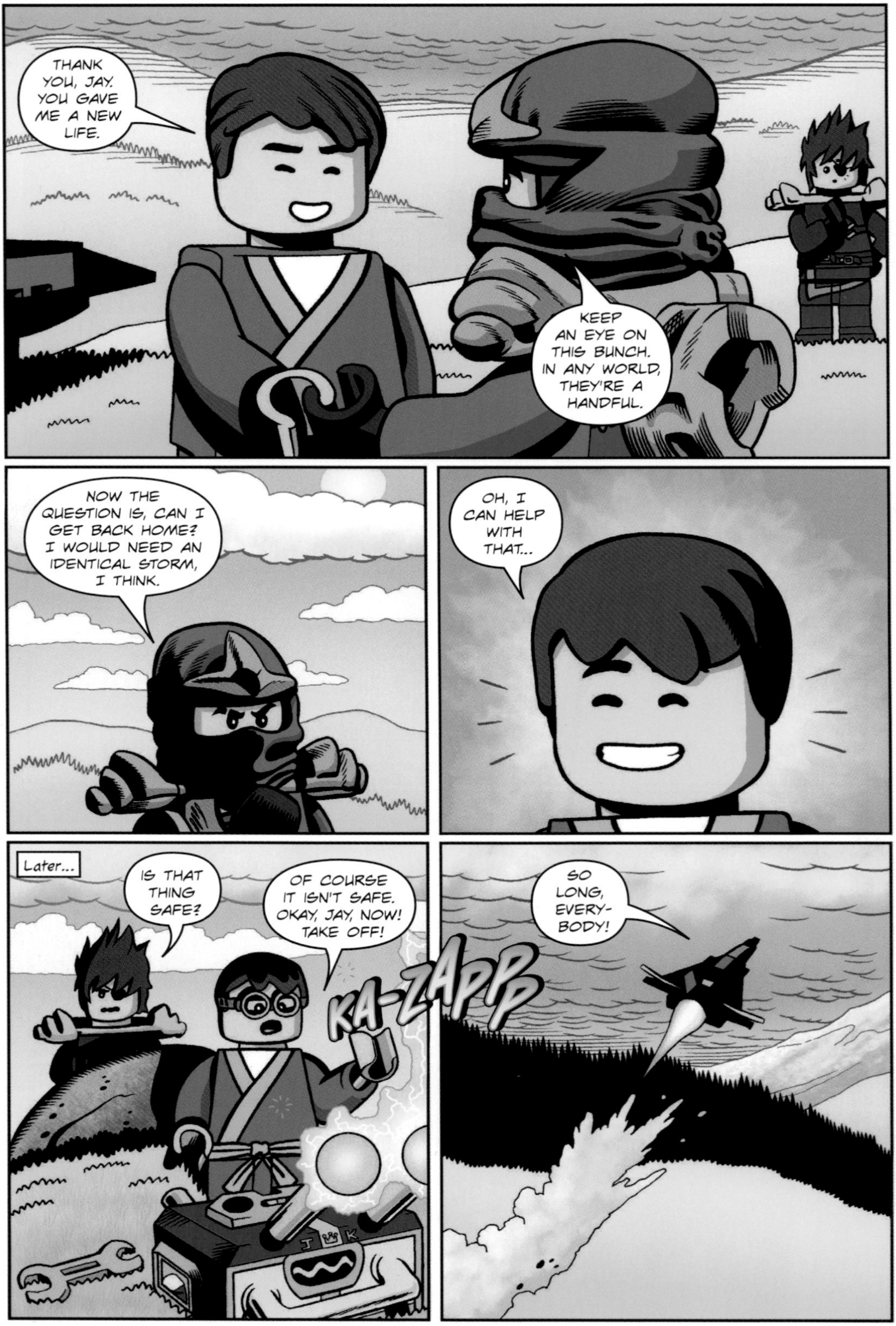
THANK YOU, JAY. YOU GAVE ME A NEW LIFE.
KEEP AN EYE ON THIS BUNCH. IN ANY WORLD, THEY'RE A HANDFUL.
NOW THE QUESTION IS, CAN I GET BACK HOME? I WOULD NEED AN IDENTICAL STORM, I THINK.
OH, I CAN HELP WITH THAT...
Later...
IS THAT THING SAFE?
OF COURSE IT ISN'T SAFE. OKAY, JAY, NOW! TAKE OFF!
KA-ZAPPP
SO LONG, EVERY-BODY!

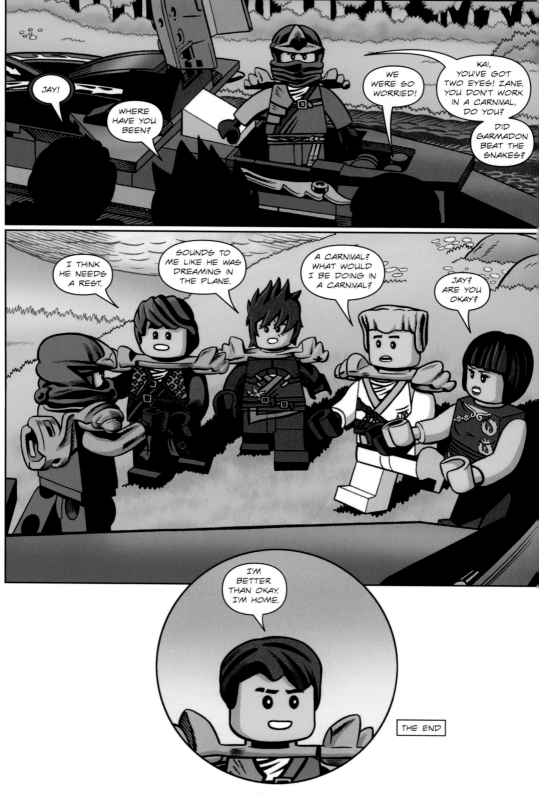

WATCH OUT FOR PAPERCUTZ™

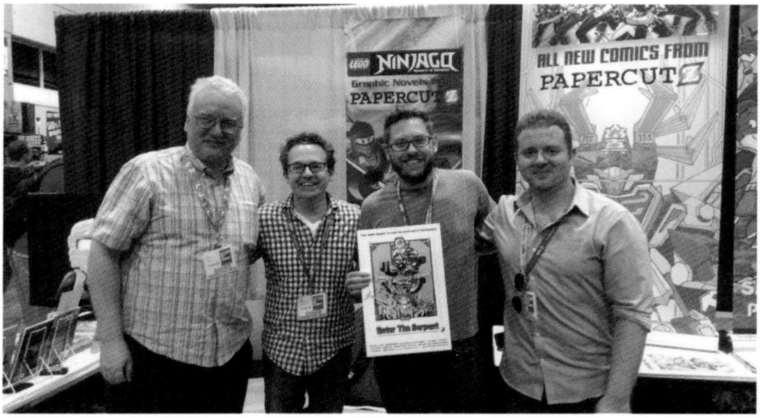
LEGO NINJAGO
PAPERCUTZ
ALL NEW COMICS FROM
PAPERCUTZ

Jim Salicrup, The Hageman Brothers, and Michael Petranek at the Papercutz Booth at the San Diego Comic-Con.

Welcome you to the fifth, fabulous LEGO® NINJAGO graphic novel from Papercutz, the company dedicated to publishing great graphic novels for all ages. I'm Jim Salicrup, Papercutz Editor-in-Chief and snakeskin shoe-shiner. We've got lots of exciting NINJAGO-related things to talk about, so let's get right to it!

Every year since Papercutz started publishing back in 2005, we've also exhibited at the world-famous Comic-Con International: San Diego, or as it's more commonly called, the San Diego Comic-Con. Being one of the new kids on the block, we tend to get overshadowed by the older, bigger comicbook publishers and their expensive big booths, which in turn tend to get dwarfed by the really big booths brought in by various movie studios/comicbook publishers and major toy companies, toy companies such as The LEGO Group! But the show is all about the fans getting to see, and sometimes even meet, their favorite movie and TV stars, and comicbook writers and artists. And even cooler than that, getting cool free stuff available only at Comic-Con!

Well, this year, Papercutz had a couple of cool free Comic-Con exclusives, as they're called. One was an Ash-Can Edition of the upcoming NANCY DREW AND THE CLUE CREW graphic novel series, and the other was a special free LEGO NINJAGO poster, inspired by a classic martial arts movie poster, and drawn and colored by Jolyon Yates. Not only were LEGO NINJAGO fans thrilled with this surprise Papercutz premium, but even the writers of the hit LEGO Ninjago TV series, the Hageman Brothers, seemed happy with it (see photo). While we can't give each and everyone of you one of these posters, we can do the next best thing. Just go to page 64 and check out the poster everyone is talking about! It follows the special preview of LEGO NINJAGO #6 "Heart of Stone."

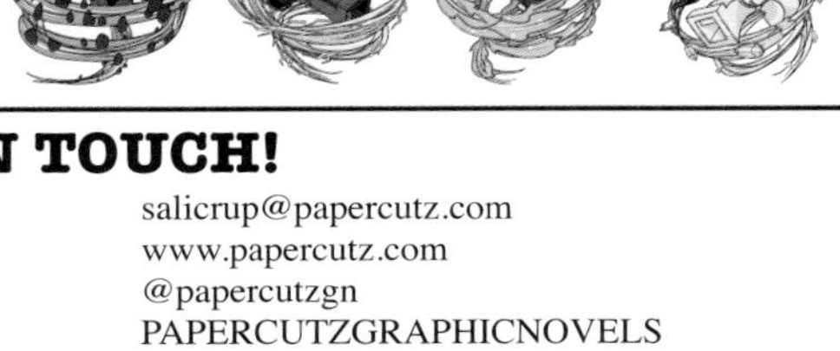

So, until next time, keep spinnin'!

Thanks,

Jim

STAY IN TOUCH!

EMAIL:	salicrup@papercutz.com
WEB:	www.papercutz.com
TWITTER:	@papercutzgn
FACEBOOK:	PAPERCUTZGRAPHICNOVELS
SNAIL MAIL:	Papercutz, 160 Broadway, Suite 700, East Wing, New York, NY 10038

Don't Miss LEGO® NINJAGO #6 "Heart of Stone"!

Enter The Serpent

The ultimate brick masterpiece! Lavishly produced on location in the world of LEGO® Ninjago!

KAI JAY COLE AND ZANE IN "ENTER THE SERPENT" CO-STARRING SENSEI WU AND INTRODUCING LLOYD GARMADON   WRITTEN BY GREG FARSHTEY   DIRECTED BY JOLYON YATES

VISUAL EFFECTS BY JAYJAY JACKSON   DIALOGUE COACH BRYAN SENKA   LINE PRODUCER MICHAEL PETRANEK   WEAPONS CONSULTANT JESSE POST   EDITED BY JIM SALICRUP   EXECUTIVE PRODUCER HELLE REIMERS HOLM-JORGENSEN

PRODUCED BY TERRY NANTIER   A LEGO NINJAGO PRODUCTION IN ASSOCIATION W PAPERCUTZ   LEGO, THE LEGO LOGO, THE BRICK AND KNOB CONFIGURATIONS AND THE MINIFIGURE ARE TRADEMARKS OF THE LEGO GROUP. ©2012 THE LEGO GROUP. PRODUCED BY PAPERCUTZ UNDER LICENSE FROM THE LEGO GROUP.

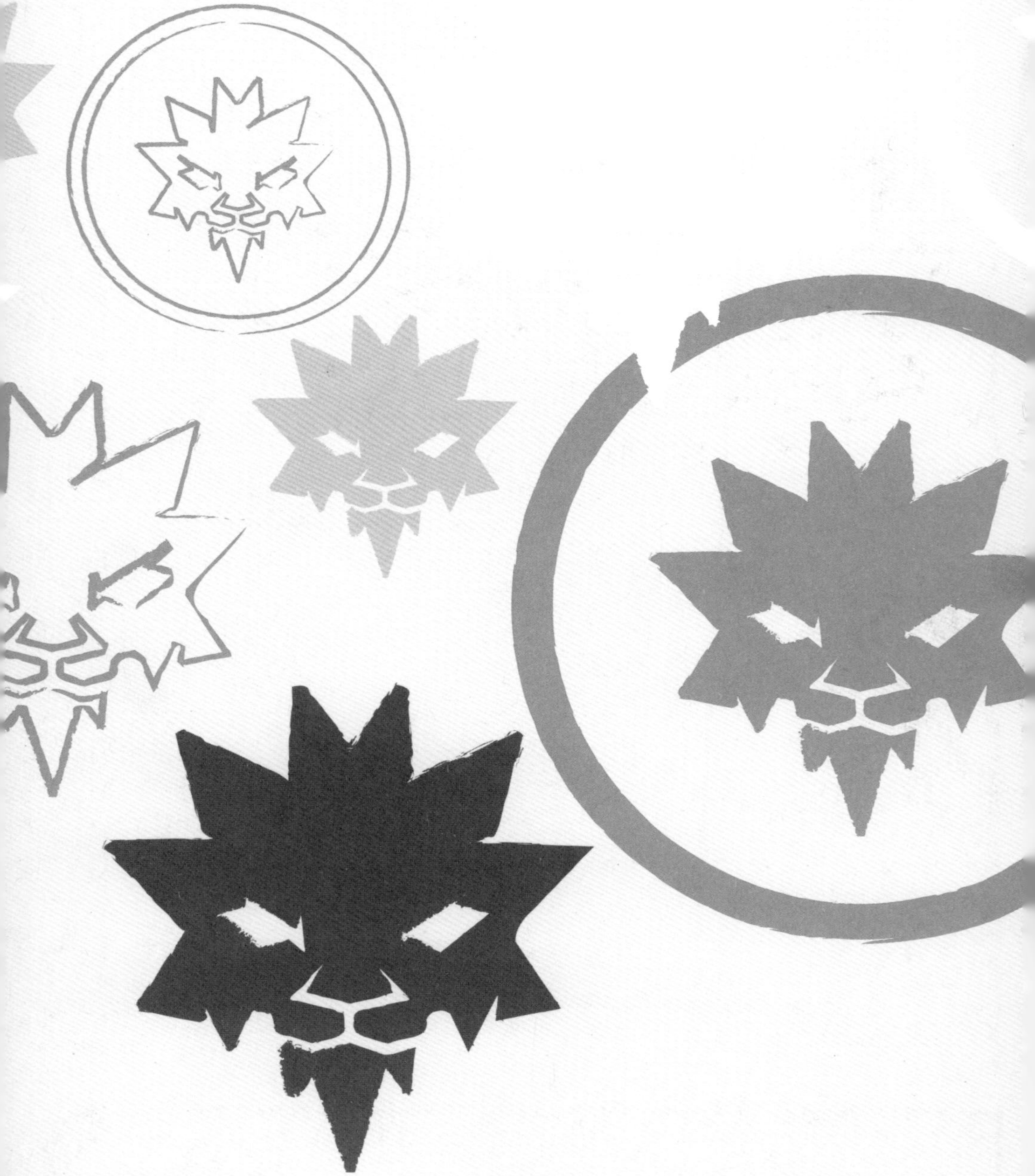